Dedic

This book is dedicated to every person who felt like they were on their own…. no one to tell their dreams, fears and darkest secrets. You have YOURSELF and as long as you have you and God you will never be alone.

The Connect's Wife

What does love feel like? Is love intended to be comfortable, to make you feel better, to hold you at night, and never tell you any lies? Is love intended to keep you warm, to make you cry, to make you smile? Must love only come after sex? Why does love have a time limit; it seems to expire after too much bullshit has occurred. Love does crazy things to us; it causes us to think too much and say things we do not really mean to say. Love can be categorized into seasons, and as the seasons change, so do people. Love will have you feeling warm as a summer day then mad and cold like a winter morning. Alternatively, love can have you embracing life and smiling at everything wrong and right. In the fall, leaves fall and I'm convinced that no two leaves are the same. So what do you do when you think you're in love and nothing can ever go wrong then all of a sudden something clicks? Am I settling? This is not love. This is not who I really want to be with. I just enjoy your sex or I just like you because you take care of me and do sweet things. I do not even think you are handsome. I cannot see myself with you, not even next week. Let me tell you what real love is. It does not see faces; real love attracts the heart. It keeps the mind, body and soul intact. Many people confuse love and lust all the time; those two are not the same. Real love does not hurt and if it does hurt, it does not hurt repeatedly. Real love is confident and it does not have to be questioned. Real love is something that everyone should get the chance to experience at least for one season in his or her lifetime. It is not fair if you do not.

Introduction

Farren Walters didn't know whose presence she entered when she met her soon to be husband. She was unaware of his lifestyle. A man of his caliber was way out of her reach, yet he chose her anyway. Christian Knight was a man that people only dreamed about in their sleep. Petty hustlers admired him off the strength of stories they heard in the hood. You could walk past Christian Knight in the mall and not know that he was "The Connect". Real men moved in silence. Wealth is quiet, rich is flashy. Christian Knight was more than a man that supplied the streets with the work. He was a mogul, a self-made billionaire who found comfort, peace and joy in the arms of Farren, a woman almost ten years younger than he was. Many people never expected him to settle down or to be so open with his affection. Despite what he heard about her, he chose her to wear his last name and to become, "The Connect's Wife".

con·nect

kəˈnekt/

Connect has been defined as "bringing together or into contact so that a real or notional link is established, joining together so as to provide access and communication or being linked to a power or water supply".

Chapter 1

"We tend to ignore the signs and wonders, when they're usually right in front of our face."

"Ms. Walters, glad you could join us." Nick Connor, head of the DEA, stood up and shook Farren's hand as she walked into a meeting she was completely unprepared for and knew absolutely nothing about. "I would say thank you, but I'm unsure of what this meeting is about," Farren replied. She did not believe in beating around the bush, or playing games.

Farren was confident in her work; she knew she performed well and always crossed her t's and dotted her i's. If an error was made or there was a loophole in any of her cases, she would be extremely disappointed in herself. For the past ten years, she worked her way up the legal ladder, working her ass off to be the best attorney she could be. She always stayed the extra hours, grinded way past the midnight hour, was the first to enter the office and the last to leave.

She was never certain whether it was the color of her skin or the fact that the money she made off of cases simply went to charities and nonprofits she supported around the cities of Philadelphia and New York. Farren did not socialize in the office, did not believe in catching a drink after a long day of depositions, or even popping champagne after she won cases that were worth millions of dollars. She took her lunch at the same time every day and never invited anyone to go with her. Farren handled her business and she handled it well. She was the mother of three beautiful children and the proud wife to Christian Knight. "Have a seat, let's chat. How is your family?" Another person asked.

Farren's head snapped back. "Cut to the bullshit, if you wanted to hire me you would have contacted my office, so how can I help you, sir?" Farren sat her Celine purse, iPhone and Blackberry on the counter, and tapped her perfectly manicured fingernails on the wooden table. Her ten-carat wedding ring and Cartier band glimmered, which was a "just because gift" from her husband and best friend of fifteen years. Before she even entered the room, her Bond fragrance and Dior pumps, clicking and clacking against the tiled floor, warned the federal agents that Mrs. Knight had entered the building.

At forty years old, she worked hard as hell as a commercial attorney at one of the top firms in New York. She drove an hour and a half to work every day, waking up at 5 a.m. to run with her husband and see her children off to school. Farren was a proud soccer mom, Girl Scout volunteer, and a very active Delta in her local graduate chapter; she was a woman who wore many hats. She did not waste time on nothingness. In her life, every second of the day was cherished and important to her.

One folder was placed in front of her. "How about you open this and you tell us what we need to know, and you just might make it home before dinner to feed Carren, Michael, and Noel," the agent smirked at her. Farren was shocked, but her face remained stone. She knew the game and she knew it well. As bad as these men probably wanted to see her crack, they would not.

She picked up the folder, stood to her feet, closed her suit jacket and simply said, "As soon as I review these documents, I will give you a call."

"We need to talk to you today," the agent stated. "Let her go, she will be calling soon. I know her kind," the boss said in a matter-of-fact tone. Farren offered a warm smile, and walked coolly to her Range Rover. She could barely get in her car and out of the parking lot fast enough; her hands were shaking and she was beginning to panic. With the swipe of her finger, she unlocked her phone and dialed "Hubby" in her favorites. "Babe, you're calling early? You must want some more from this morning," her husband said jokingly upon answering the phone, only today there was nothing to laugh about.

"Baby, I can't talk over the phone, just tell me where you are," Farren yelled.

"What's wrong, Farren?" Christian asked. He was always concerned with his family's well-being.

"I can't talk over the phone, where the fuck are you?" she asked. Her line clicked, informing her that her assistant was calling.

"My office; slow down because I know you're speeding." He disconnected the call as Farren clicked over. "Farren Knight," she answered. Even in the midst of everything she knew she was soon to face, she still had to remain corporate.

"Some roses came for you, Mrs. Knight," her assistant, Dolly, reported cheerfully. "I won't be in today, sweetie, just put them on my desk. Can you handle everything today? I don't want any calls or emails unless it's an emergency," Farren stated. She already knew Dolly wouldn't mind. Because of Farren, Dolly was able to take care of her two young daughters, live in a gated neighborhood and attend school. "Yes ma'am." Dolly knew not to ask any questions, just to do as Farren said. Farren did not tell her enough how much she appreciated her and looked to her as a daughter, or even younger sister.

Farren pulled up to her husband's office and took the elevator to the seventh floor where she was greeted by his receptionist. She knew she was probably giving Christian head from time to time, but today she wasn't in the mood to roll her eyes and toss her neck; she needed to see her husband. Christian looked as if he was waiting on her to get there. She slammed the door and threw the folder on his desk.

"What the fuck have you been doing!" she yelled with tears in her eyes and mascara running down her face. She snatched her Prada shades off so fast, the handle broke. Christian saw the anger in her eyes; it was mixed in with fear.

He sat down and reviewed the contents; this information had to come from a trusted source. However, he did not trust easily so who was running their mouth? For the first time in years, Christian admitted to himself he was worried. He leaned back in his Italian leather chair, and began and rubbing a hand over his face. "Do you know what happens to niggas who get greedy? They go to jail," she yelled.

Christian's dirt had finally caught up to him. Over the past few years, he had made millions of dollars. "Farren, this is all incorrect,

I promise you baby," he looked in her eyes. His eyes never lied to her. She always believed him, even during their first encounter, which was her second year of law school.

• •

Circa 1986

Farren

"I'm sorry sir; we don't have these in a thirteen. I'd advise you to try the twelve and a half, because this designer tends to make his shoes bigger than normal," I said, offering the older man the shoe, which he hesitantly took. If I did not know anything else in life, I was confident in shoes. I lived, breathed and was completely infatuated with shoes. My closet held clothes, but shoes definitely ruled every square foot of my small home.

"Hi, is there anything I can help you with today? And let me say that we have 55% off of all Giuseppe Zanotti sandals until next Friday;

however, sizes are very limited," I greeted a customer, offering a warm smile. "Nah sweetie, I'm here to bring back all of this." He pointed to more than nineteen pairs of different designer shoes. "Is it safe to ask why you are returning this limited edition Chanel sneakers? I wanted these," I asked, as I scanned a few of the boxes. "My fiancé was cheating. I don't even care for this type of stuff - she did, so I want my money back," he stated sternly. "Well let me buy these Chanel sneakers from you," I said jokingly. "Look ma' you can have them, let's just make this process smooth because I don't have any of the receipts," he said. "I'll see what can be returned and whatever can't, I know some people who will get these from you, like today." "Alright, come on ma'am, I can't be in here all day. What's your name?" he asked.

"The name is Farren. Please follow me this way." Surprisingly everything returned and I issued him more than $5,200. He casually rolled the money up in a rubber band as if it were nothing to him. "Here's my card, call me when you get off so we can link up and you get these shoes." He handed me a matte black crisp card with "KNIGHT CONSTRUCTION" which also included an email and phone number. "Will do. Thank you."

The rest of the day went by pretty slow. I was so ready to get off work. I had been here since 7 a.m. preparing the store for another long day of sales. I hate sales. People who normally don't shop come in with a million questions, trying on a million shoes and even with the discount, they still choose not to buy anything. As manager, I preferred to only work with frequent buyers, but my love for shoes keeps me in the midst of all types of customers.

At night I worked as a bartender at a Tapas restaurant located in downtown Philly. Bills had to be paid, and I was already knee deep in student loans because I was finishing my third year in law school. I caught the subway to my BMW. As bad as I needed to get to the gym before it was time to work, I wanted those shoes more than anything. I fished through my satchel for his business card, and then proceeded to dial his number.

"Wassup," he answered.

"Hi Mr. Knight, this is Farren from Nordstrom's. I just got off work and was wondering where can we meet up?" I asked.

"Meet me at the courtyard gym, I'm here hooping."

"Oh my goodness, that's perfect, that's my gym! I'll text you after my workout." I rushed in the ladies room, changed into my Nike leggings and sports bra, and re-laced my sneaks. With Beyoncé blazing through my headphones, I was in a zone as I ran three miles.

Christian

"Who in the hell is that?" my home boy asked as we dropped our sweaty towels in the basket. I glanced over in his direction, and there she was…. the lil' youngin' from the mall. Honey-golden skin glistened in the sweetest sweat I ever seen drip down someone's face.

Her abs were toned and her arms were defined; she looked good and in shape without appearing too athletic. Her hips were wide and her breasts moved up and down in a slow raving motion. You could tell she was in deep thought from the way her tongue ran across the nicest set of teeth I'd ever seen on a black woman. Her manicured hands brushed the top of her forehead, and the sweat seemed to fall off suddenly. This lady just happened to be a goddess. I couldn't stop staring. She must have noticed, because her pace slowed and suddenly came to a complete halt.

She dabbed her stomach and arms with a towel and when she bent over to retrieve her belongings, me and my good friends, all got an eagle's view of the roundest apple ever. That ass had to have been hiding in her corporate work attire, or I was too agitated this morning to notice anything. I was hell bent on getting all Miranda's shit out my house by the end of the week.

She walked over slowly but surely. "Hi, Mr. Knight," she said.

"Stop calling me that, I'm Chris. You come here all the time? I've never seen you here."

"I'm here three times a week," she replied.

"Well it's paying off, you look good as hell," my home boy Greg told her.

"Thanks. I have about 30 more pounds to lose."

"You don't need to lose anything else," I told her. I liked my women thick in the right places and slim on top. Damn, I'm getting ahead of myself. She's not my woman!

"You don't know what I look like naked." She grabbed what she thought was pounds of fat but to me, was amazing.

"Come on; let me get your shoes."

"Thank you so much. I wanted these so bad, but we aren't allowed to hold anything longer than three days, and at the time I just couldn't afford them," she said.

"I know how that can be. Well consider them a gift," I told her, as we walked to my Porsche truck.

"I really appreciate it. Find me next time you're in the store; I'm over the shoe department," she told me as she prepared to go to her car. "Will do," I replied.

I watched her locate a black BMW, pulling off shortly thereafter. That would not be my last time seeing Ms. Farren but until then, I had other shit to handle.

"Yo... I'm about to go home, hit the shower, and I'll hit y'all when I'm heading that way." I honked at my home boys before I pulled off and headed to the place I lay my head. My five-bedroom, three-story abode, was my pride and glory. I built my home from the ground up and designed every inch of it myself. I built this home with only four other trusted people. It took years, but it was the fruits of my labor, and I was damn proud of myself.

At thirty-five years old, a college graduate from Brown University with an Architecture degree, I sought out to be the number one designer in Philadelphia and New York. I worked hard my whole life, which is why I'm so frugal now. My parents weren't wealthy, they were honest hard workers. I balanced a 4.0 GPA and basketball all through high school so my parents wouldn't have to struggle with sending me to college. My sisters and I all became college graduates. Five years ago, I told my parents to retire early and enjoy life. With no children and no wife, I was free to travel whenever I wanted and come home as late as I pleased.

Unfortunately, I was Mr. Homebody himself; I never went out because I didn't like being on the scene. I am a businessman who closes million dollar renovation deals, weekly. My business and my brand mean everything to me.

On top of my successful company, I was a self-made billionaire. The last time I talked to my accountant, he reported that my total income for the month was an estimated sixty-five thousand. I had reached my peak of success. My time was no longer spent whipping it up and breaking it down. I spent my mornings running around my estate, and drinking coffee imported from Bolivia. Guys that hugged the block didn't even know who I was, and I planned on keeping it that way. My name was irrelevant; my identity was to remain a mystery. There was no way anyone could get in touch with me if they wanted to be put on. I didn't need security guards and I had no need to carry heavy weaponry. I was safe and sound in my home.

Being "The Connect" came with more ups than downs. I was content stacking money every day, investing every dollar. Greed leads to a person's downfall, so this wouldn't be my life forever. Yet, the hustle in me just wouldn't come to an end. My other businesses and career proved to be successful, but there was nothing like the thrill of being able to make decisions with the snap of your finger. An army of more than one-hundred loyal men, who only knew what I stood for not what I looked like, placed a thrill in me that I couldn't explain. Being "The Connect" was ravishing; it was an extra boost of energy when I woke up. The buzzing of my phone snapped me out of thoughts.

"What up ma." I answered my personal line as I waited on my water to reach a temperature I was comfortable with.

"Christian baby, that girl had me on the phone for two hours saying you won't let her explain, talking my damn ear off. Her mother called and said this is an embarrassment to their family. Now what you want me to tell these folks... keep calling me meddling in your business." I smiled.

My precious mother was old school. She respected my wishes and never questioned me about any decisions I made because her and my father raised us right. My sisters and I have never been arrested, and they weren't whores. In fact, Courtney just received her PhD in Research, and she's married with three children. Chloe, who chose to be a stay-at-home mom and work as an administrative assistant for me from time to time, married a travel sales agent and had two sons. Both of them turned out wonderful.

"Ma, I'm not stunting that girl or her mama. The wedding will not be happening so she needs to stop calling you. She wasn't calling you before, so she doesn't need to start now," I told her as I tossed my boxers and socks.

"Christian, I have minded my business and your father hasn't said much, but people make mistakes. She said you spent so much time in your office and she felt neglected, but that doesn't take away from her being the woman you can marry and bear your children. I want you to be happy, son." She was so concerned but there wasn't a need.

"Ma, if I can keep my joint in my pants when I'm around beautiful women all the time, then I expect the same in return. She was out of my league anyway; she had no ambition, nothing going on. I'm not going to be the only one working hard in this house while she sits back and appreciates nothing; telling me she doesn't wear the same shoes twice... I grew up with three pairs of shoes!" I found myself getting mad all over again. "Mama, I'm call you later," I said, before I disconnected the call.

I felt my anger rising as I slammed my hand against the wall. Miranda stripped me of love; she took everything she could from me, mentally. It started off so great, then she started demanding more; always wanting rough sex, she quit her job, begged me for a ring – damn it, it just wasn't meant to be. As I washed the basketball funk off of me, I reflected to the day I asked her to leave my home and leave my ring.

"Hi baby, I'm home!" She pranced her lying, cheating ass across my marble floors. I was having me a drink and smoking a blunt. "Wassup," I responded. She dropped shopping

bags at my feet, and hopped in my lap, flicking ashes all over my t-shirt. "Damn girl!" I hissed. She giggled, "Sorry baby. I've missed you. I've been calling you all day." She batted her false eyelashes and slung her thirty-inch weave over her shoulder, and prepared to kiss my lips.

I quickly grabbed her neck. "You think you're going to kiss me with the same lips you been suckin' that nigga dick with?" Her eyes damn near popped out of her head. I saw that the pressure was a little too much and I let her go with so much force she fell back on the floor, onto my white mink carpet. "You can leave with what you came with.....NOTHING. A cab is waiting on you to take you back to your mother's car," I stated, before I prepared to leave the room.

"Christian, our wedding is in two months," she yelled.

"What wedding?" I turned around and asked.

"Christian you will not embarrass me!"

"Embarrass? Miranda I'm having a lunch meeting and I see you leaving a hotel with some young nigga. I'm the one embarrassed and I wasn't even the one who caught you, Jeremiah did." My business partner hated her anyway so it was icing on the cake for him, but for me, it was a stab through my heart.

"You're assuming that was me," she cried.

"Don't insult my intelligence baby, just go on and leave. I told you in the beginning I'll give you the world if only you respect me and keep it real."

"I did keep it real Christian, I can't live without you," she wailed.

"Miranda, I gave you all of me; don't play me like a simple nigga. You fucked up, you'll get over it," I smiled. I was hurting on the inside, but her ass would never know that.

"Please don't leave me." She cried so much, her makeup was completely ruined.

"Miranda, get the fuck out. I will not ask you again. My number is already changed and the locks will be changed, too. I'll call around and find you a job, that's the least I can do being that you didn't plan on losing your fantastic life in one day," I told her as I helped her to the door and to the cab.

"I would take your card, but I already had my assistant cancel the shit. There is no way you had me paying for hotel rooms this whole time, like I'm a sucker. Here's one-hundred....nah, twenty dollars to get something to eat with!" I slammed the cab door and went back to my home, happy that chapter closed before it could get started.

My phone buzzing snapped me out of my trance, and I was happy that it did. Miranda was a closed chapter in my life and I wanted to keep it that way. I departed from my shower and answered the text message; it was a picture from Farren.

"Too thirsty to wear these... I'm stepping out in these tonight☺." She had on a black blazer, white wife beater and green jeans with the new sneakers. That definitely caused a smile to form across my face.

"Looking fly, ma. Where are you headed tonight?"

"My second job." *Damn she a hard worker.*

"And where might that be?"

"Two fifty-five! Come through, drinks on me!"

"Fa sho'."

I threw on a pair of army fatigue pants and a white t-shirt. This May weather was nippy but not quite, so my Timbs went perfect, along with my rose gold Rolex and Cartier bracelet.

After playing pool with the fellas, I headed solo over to 255. I found an empty seat at the bar, and flagged the young lady from earlier down. I couldn't remember her name...Farrah...Felicia... my mind was boggled.

"Uh, excuse me. Can I get a Henny and coke?" I shot my new friend a smile.

"No you cannot, sir, try this." She had concocted something together.

"I don't like clear." I pushed it back to her and lit a cigar.

"You're supposed to always try something once." She winked and walked off.

Oh what the hell, I thought to myself and surprisingly, that shit was good. "Make me another one." I tossed her a hundred dollar bill.

She looked at it and handed it back. "You're good." She fixed me another drink and went to tend to her other customers. The vibe in here was nice; I would definitely be back.

I looked down at my phone to see an unknown number calling, and immediately I declined.

"Go on and clock out, I'm hungry," I told her as I put my cigar out and placed my shades back on. "Who do you think you are?" she asked with her hands on her hips. "The owner, so come on."

I forgot about this little place I'd purchased a few years ago. I'll be pulling the numbers first thing in the a.m. to see how much money this place was making me.

"I'm kind of faded, ma. You drive my car good, ya hear."

"You always hop random girls in your car?" she asked, declining and opting to drive her car, as we hit the highway.

I rubbed her thigh. "Ain't no way you random... I'm feeling you." I knew I was a little drunk because I'm usually not so open with my feelings.

"You don't even know me and you're too damn old for me," she laughed.

"Damn, how old I look?" I asked her, as I pulled her visor down and scanned over my face. I had a few grey strands in my beard but besides that, no wrinkles were evident. I was six-foot-five, dark skinned and I found myself very attractive.

"Forty," she stated firmly.

"I'm thirty five, how old are you?" I asked.

"Twenty-six."

"Shit, you ain't twenty-one your damn self; you're pushing thirty," I joked.

"Oh my goodness, don't remind me. I hate being grown!" she hissed.

"Embrace life. Pull up in that Waffle House," I told her.

She parked and tossed her gun in her purse. I just looked at her. "What? Your fiancé might come in here raising hell and I'mma have to pop her," she joked.

"Nah baby, you ain't gotta worry about none of that, but I'm glad one of us is strapped," I told her, as I groped her waist and held the door at the same time.

Over breakfast, we had a three-hour conversation that led to everything. She loved 255 and definitely had some ideas on revisions. She didn't like management, and I was embarrassed because I don't even remember who managed that property; it was more of an investment than anything. Her smile was contagious; every time she smiled, I found myself smiling. Every time she held her stomach and laughed, I laughed, too. After I paid our tab, we prepared to leave. "Sorry our first date was at the Waffle House," I joked.

"First, this wasn't a date and second, I'm from the hood. I love me some Waffle House," she reassured me.

"So when can I take you on a real date?" I asked her. She shook her head. "We're on two different levels."

"I didn't ask you that."

"We will see. Now come on. I have to get home, I have class in the a.m.," she said and pulled my arm.

"You're in school and you work two jobs?" I asked, once we were back on the highway, headed back to my truck.

I couldn't help but to stare at her; she was beyond beautiful. And the fact that she was able to hold my attention without me being on my phone, was a plus in my book. She was pretty amazing, and I wanted more of her in every aspect.

"How else you think I'm paying for law school?"

"Damn ma, I love that shit. Yo, I'm proud of you. I was the same way, man. I would get out of school at 3:30, go to practice, do my homework, and then go cut grass. And in college, I used to write papers so I wouldn't have to ask my parents for any extra money. Both of my sisters wanted to pledge and they always needed new clothes and shit," I opened up to her.

"You have sisters and they're Greek? What did they pledge? I'm a Delta," she stated proudly, and pointed to the elephant pendant in her car.

"Wow, so are they," I told her.

"I'll have to meet my sorors one day," she smiled.

"I love my family; I have four nephews and one niece."

"I or my sister has yet to have children. She's finishing up nursing school and I have two years left in law school."

"It takes five years? I had a friend that finished in three."

"I'm working two jobs, so I'm part-time. I wish I could go full-time so I could be done, but I got bills and stuff," her voice trailed off.

"Here's your vehicle," she smiled.

"Call me tomorrow when you get out of class; let me take you to lunch," I said, as I held her hand and kissed it.

"I have to work," she said.

"Call off," I told her.

"I can't do that. I don't work Friday night so I'll call you then."

"No, still call me tomorrow. Goodnight." I hopped out before she could answer. She didn't pull off until I started my engine. I was taking notice of all the little things, making me dig her a little more.

I rode through the city and thanked God for the come-up. I struggled my whole life, not necessarily physically, but mentally. Riding through my old hood humbled me; it was something I did when I couldn't sleep. I came from nothing to something. I went from sweeping the floor in the corner store to buying the empty space next door and turning it into a laundromat. I remember when I first made the decision to get into the game.

It wasn't an easy decision. I was a smart kid who even went to church every Sunday faithfully, 'cause moms ain't play that. But I wanted more. I was tired of counting pennies together. I hated saving up money just to get the newest sneakers. In college, I was on my own.

My daddy told me when he and my mother dropped me off, *"I got you here boy, now make us proud."* In so many words, he was telling me to handle my business because they had two other mouths to feed.

I wanted more in life and I didn't stop until I got to a certain level of comfort. Even now with multi-million dollar accounts, I still wanted more. My happiness was more important than the riches, and I knew it was time for me to remove the hurt and pain I experienced from my break up with Miranda.

I was a quiet man and didn't speak on my feelings. Somehow along the way of me climbing the ladder of success, I allowed Gucci and Fendi to replace "I love you" and "I care for you". In my next relationship, I wanted more of a spiritual connection; not on any sucker shit, but just a real bond with my partner. I wanted my cold nights to be warm, and Farren was the face that popped up when I thought of the person I imagined spending my spare time with.

Tonight was one of those nights where I didn't want to be alone, but I wasn't in the mood to be in the strip club or hang around my niggas. It was nothing for me to call up some quick ass, but Farren Walters was on my mind.

"Are you up?" I asked Farren once I heard her sweet voice.

"Yes, what's wrong?" she asked.

"Nothing, I just want to take you to get breakfast in the morning before you start your day," I said, making up something up quick.

"Okay. I wake up very early, like five in the morning"

"Me too, I'll call you in a few hours"

"Okay, get some rest. See you soon," she said coolly and hung the phone up.

After hearing her voice and confirming plans for the morning, I was able to turn my vehicle around and head home. I barely slept as it was. After working out, showering and looking over some potential investments, I sat in deep thought in my living room. I didn't want to be alone forever. The ringing of the phone broke my concentration.

"Are you up?" Farren asked.

"Yeah I haven't been to sleep. Where would you like to meet?"

"Hmm...it's this coffee spot on 14th, are you familiar?

"No, I'm not' just send me the address. I'm on the way," I told her. With the phone to my ear, I slid on my Nike's and headed out the door. Thirty minutes later, I parallel parked and entered the tiny, yet intimate coffee shop, and scanned the room for Farren. I spotted her waving her hand in my peripheral. "Good morning." I kissed her cheek, and I could have sworn I saw her blush.

"How are you? Why am I asking you that and I just saw you six hours ago," she laughed, and sipped her tea.

"I couldn't get you off of my mind," I admitted and stared right into her eyes.

Her eyes did not waver from mine, either. "That's good to know," she smirked.

"Smooth... I'll give you that", I told her.

"So what's on your agenda today, Mr. Knight?"

"I want it to be you, but you're busy."

"For you, I just might make an exception," she smiled. *Gosh her smile was everything.*

"Do that for me and I promise you won't regret it. It's really something about you..."

"It is?" she asked, flipping her hair, her confidence filling the room. She wasn't shy or timid, nor was she conceited and pompous. It was a balance. Her persona matched mine perfectly.

I was a grown-ass man, flirting and blushing at six in the morning with a girl years younger than me. I had to gain some control over this situation.

"So what is it exactly that you do? Your card just said Knight Construction, and I've since found out that you own 255," she stated. When she asked last night, I brushed the subject off.

"To sum it up, I buy small businesses and make them pop. What do you like to eat?" I asked her, wanting to know as much about her as possible.

"I love seafood and steak."

"So tonight we can go to Ocean Prime. I want you dressed up though - no sneakers. Let me see you in some heels," I said.

"I got you, boo."

Our conversation flowed so easily, we had lost track of time; it had swiftly passed us by. We sat at the coffee shop up until she had to leave.

"I'll see you around seven. Are you sure you don't want me to come get you?" I asked her again.

"I like driving my own car," she stated firmly.

"I respect it. We will text and touch bases around four. Enjoy your day," I told her.

"I can't get a hug?" she asked.

Of course boo. You can get a hug, a kiss, some dick - whatever you want, is what I thought to myself but instead I said, "Come here," and pulled her into a bear hug, holding her waist close to mine for a few seconds.

I kissed her cheek and watched her get in her car safely before getting into my truck and heading back home. I had suddenly became sleepy.

Farren

Tonight was me and Christian's first date and I had no idea on what to wear. It's not that I was nervous or anything, but I wanted to impress him. It was obvious after only one full day of meeting we were crushing on each other.

He was on a different level then me; traveling often, handling business, and owning several businesses. I liked the fact his conversation was well-rounded. We discussed everything from politics to music, clothes and everything else under the sun.

Christian had already texted me twice to confirm our "date". He wanted me to know that this was *definitely* a date. I stood in my closet butt-naked, dripping wet on my tiptoes, to pull down a shoebox that held these black ostrich pumps. In the process, two other shoeboxes had come tumbling down on my head. "Shit," I hissed.

After a few more minutes on contemplating over the perfect outfit, I slid into a black dress from Express that fit me like glove. The thin spaghetti straps had tiny speckles of gold on them, the abdomen area was sheer and the dress stopped at my knees. I felt like a goddess. I wasn't a fan of makeup, so I only added eyeliner and a little mascara to my eyelashes. I dabbed my favorite fragrance behind my ears and wrists, and placed the black ostrich pumps on my feet. I then pressed my hair bone straight, and added a part in the middle.

Forty-five minutes later, I valeted my car and smoothed over my dress once more. *"Okay Farren, enjoy yourself,"* I said, giving myself a pep talk before entering the restaurant.

"Hello Ms. Walters, this way," the hostess spoke before I could even ask where Christian's table was located. It was my first time at the restaurant, but I still didn't understand why we walked past so many tables without seeing Christian. The hostess led me to the back of the restaurant and to a private elevator.

"Okay, Ms. Walters, get off on the second floor and enjoy your meal," the older lady told me with a smile.

I felt my heart beating faster once the elevator jumped and came to a complete stop. It chimed and opened all in one motion. I stuck my head out before stepping off, and I saw another door. I heard nothing.

"What are you doing?" Christian's voice suddenly appeared from nowhere.

"Shit! You scared me," I said, holding my chest.

"You look beautiful." He came closer to me and kissed my cheek and hand. "Damn... and you smell good." He gave me the once over and I was happy that he was satisfied. Something inside of me wanted to always keep a smile on his face.

"Come on, our dinner is this way. Why were you peeking over there? That's another private dinner." He took my hand and led me in the opposite direction.

"I've never been here before. It's really nice. Do you always sit up here in the private section?" I asked.

The restaurant itself was beautiful. I appreciated fine dining, good wine, live jazz and classical pieces of art. Frequent customers were allowed to rent out small rooms with your own waiter, and that's where we were having dinner.

"It depends on what mood I'm in," he answered my question.

"Is that your hair?" he asked.

"Yes it is" I told him. I was blessed with long, wild, curly and sometimes, bushy hair.

"Farren, what are your goals?" he asked.

I've never been asked that question before so it kind of caught me off guard. No one ever really showed interest in anything that I had going on.

"I want to change the world", I told him, honestly.

"And how will you do that?" he asked.

"When I get rich, I want to go back to the projects and have SAT preparation workshops for the kids, and just help them. I had to do so much on my own because I told myself I had to get out of there, and I did," I solemnly replied.

"So, what are your goals? How are you going to change the world?" he asked again, but in a different tone. He was challenging me to think. So instead of blurting out an answer, I thought long and hard before responding.

"I'm going to become a commercial attorney and I will help people who can't afford a good attorney."

"So you plan on doing a lot of pro bono cases. What about you? How will you eat or become successful if you're working for free?" he asked.

"I'm going to take other cases, too, but I don't want to forget about the people like me.... I can't forget about the people like me." He wouldn't understand because he wasn't in my shoes.

I struggled my whole life until my estranged father appeared out of nowhere. Sometimes I wish he would have stayed away because once he did start providing, it caused a huge rift between me and my sister. She went from being my best friend to my worst enemy.

"Toast to new beginnings." I lifted my wine glass and he did the same.

"Salud," Christian offered.

Dinner was amazing. I really enjoyed myself and I couldn't deny my attraction to him. We spent the entire night listening to the jazz band and drinking wine, holding each other. He was so warm the moment was more than comfortable.

"I love this dress on you. Turn around for me one more time," he said. I stood up and twirled around slowly. "So beautiful," he beamed.

"Thank you." I whispered. He made feel like a high-school girl.

His phone vibrated and it wasn't the first time throughout dinner. I noticed him clench his jaw. "I'm going to have cut this night short, I apologize, sweetie." He stood and put his suit jacket back on.

"It's okay. I really enjoyed myself. I need to go home and study anyway," I said, sipping the last of my wine.

"Text me when you get home so I can know you're tucked in safe." He kissed my cheek and jetted.

I watched him leave and wondered, what the hell this man had going on. I wasn't stupid by a long shot. I knew he was into other things besides "construction and investment properties". It was clear that he had other dealings, even if it wasn't drugs or something illegal, he had another lifestyle.

I prayed that it wasn't anything to serious that would turn me off, or away from him.

Chapter 2

Farren

Weeks had passed since my first encounter with Mr. Christian Knight. It seemed as if it were ten years ago, maybe twenty, when I met Christian instead of a few weeks ago. The time we spent together was always memorable, even though I barely seen him due to our conflicting schedules. It was as if we were in two different time zones. When I was preparing for bed, Christian would just be leaving his house. All I did was work, go to school and sleep. Even eating wasn't always on my schedule, and my weight loss was proof to that. I didn't deal with stress well and when I did stress, I felt like my life was ending.

Today had to be one of the longest days. I failed another exam due to lack of time and energy, and I could almost bet I would be repeating this semester. I left class dragging my feet, but I refused to give up on my dream of becoming a lawyer and owning my own firm. My mother had struggles her whole life, raising my sister and me, and all I want to do is make sure she is well taken care of, and me, too.

As soon as I locked the door, I placed my head on the steering wheel and cried my soul out. I was so tired of being sick and tired; tired of never having enough money to spend on me, tired of helping this person and that person, tired of failing my tests, and tired of never getting enough sleep. I met an amazing guy who I can't even enjoy spending time with, because by the time I get home from work and do my homework, every restaurant is closed and so are the movie theatres.

I'm tired of giving my all when the tunnel of success still seems so far away. I cried and cried, and cried... something had to give. I just needed to get away. I had a little money to spare and that's what I was going to do this weekend. Fuck work and fuck school; I'll get back on the grind Monday. I called Christian. My day was horrible and I just needed to hear his voice.

"Hello," Christian answered.

"Hi, how are you? Are you busy? Where are you?" I asked.

He chuckled. "Hi stranger, I'm well, I'm wrapping up my day, no I'm not busy and I'm on 43rd at one of my client's locations," he replied.

"Can I meet you there? I need a hug," I asked solemnly. "Sure lady, call me when you're outside."

After disconnecting the call, I cranked my car up and did eighty the entire ride until I reached his location. I attempted to conceal what was left of my makeup but there was no help; I still looked and felt like shit.

I smoothed out the wrinkles in my white button down shirt, and ran my hands through my hair, before getting out of the car and walking up to where he told me to meet him.

"What's wrong with you?" He placed his hand on my shoulder and pulled me back once I tried to hurry by him into his office.

"I just wanted to see you." He peeled away my Prada shades, his eyes met mine, and instantly our souls connected. The warm embrace I felt when my breast met his chest, was all I needed to let go... minutes later.

"Now talk to me, what's wrong? I haven't heard from you in a week. You don't answer the phone or anything," he stated. Christian was so handsome that I could stare into his big beautiful eyes all day.

"I'm so stressed out. It looks like I'm going to have to redo this semester, and I'm tired of taking loans out. These jobs don't pay no fuckin' money, and I'm too old to be living with my mama but the only way I'll be able to focus on school is if I give up my condo and move back in with her," I huffed and puffed.

"Do you believe in yourself?" he asked me.

I just stared at him. "Sometimes I do, but today I don't." At least I was being honest. Were my dreams too big? Did they not mirror my image?

"Don't quit; do what you gotta do. It will make you appreciate everything you earn in life because you'll know how hard you worked for it," he told me.

I nodded my head. "I just came to see you. I didn't want you to think I had forgotten about you. It's not just you I'm not talking to; I'm not talking to anyone. I don't even know why I pay a cell phone bill since I never have time to use it," I said, attempting to make a joke.

"Your ambition and that pretty smile of yours is what reeled me in." He kissed me on the forehead then the nose before landing on my lips.

I pulled back. "Let me get out of here. I need to go pack a bag. I need to clear my head, so I'm headed to Atlanta for the weekend," I told him.

"Why Atlanta?" he asked.

"Going there, I won't have to pay for a hotel or a rental; a few of my line sisters are there," I told him.

"You don't want to go to a beach?" he asked.

"Shit I wish, but that's not in my budget, sir," I replied.

"I can use a getaway; let's go to St. Thomas," he said with a smirk.

"Are you for real?"

"Yes, let me take you away and show you how you're really supposed to be treated," he told me.

"Let me go take a shower and call my mama and I need to run in the mall and get a swimsuit," I ranted.

He pulled me back again. "No, all you need to do is call your mother and tell her you're with me and we will be back on Monday morning, while I book us a flight."

"I don't deserve you," I whispered.

"Well I guess we don't deserve each other," he smiled and kissed my hand.

Needless to say, I damn sure wasn't expecting all of this, but I planned on enjoying myself for the next two days because I desperately needed a vacation.

After an hour or two of Christian and I wrapping up a few loose ends before we left for a trip, we sat in the airport, holding hands, and preparing our restless minds for a three-day getaway from all the stress and madness that life had to offer.

"Have you ever flown before?" Christian asked me while we waited on the airline to tell us we could board the plane.

"Of course I have."

"Hey, it never hurts to ask."

"There are a few places that I want to visit one day," I said.

"Like where, if you don't mind me asking?"

I closed my eyes and relished on the idea. "Hmm...Africa, Paris, Costa Rica and the Cayman Islands, for sure."

"The Cayman Islands is real nice," he said, alerting me to the fact he has traveled there before.

"I believe you," I smiled and squeezed his hand.

"You are so beautiful," he said, looking into my eyes as he spoke. It was something about the way he spoke to me.

"Now boarding first-class passengers for Flight 119...Attention now boarding first-class passengers for Flight 119," the announcement came over the intercom.

"That's us boo, come on," Christian stood and held his hand out for me to join him in line.

After scanning our passports and placing our carry-on luggage into the overhead, we were buckled in and preparing for takeoff. "I'm so tired..." I tried to contain my yawns.

"Get some rest love. When you wake up, we will be in paradise."

I kissed his cheek and rest my head on his shoulder. Before I knew it I was knocked out!

Nine hours later, after we settled in and took baths, our first night in St. Thomas was spent eating Latin food with my hands and dancing with foreigners. In a matter of time, I had downed back-to-back shots of tequila. Christian held my hand as we walked along the beach. "I needed this," I told him.

"The trip or the vodka, because baby you're wasted." He laughed as he inhaled and exhaled on something very exotic.

"Both," I smiled.

"Can I ask you something?" he said.

"Sure baby."

"Why are you alone?"

I waited to ponder over the definition of 'alone'. "I enjoy being by myself; do I come off as lonely? Oh my goodness, I hope not. I am content; I am not looking or expecting anything from anyone... I'm just living my life." I hope that's the answer he was looking for.

"So you don't see yourself getting married or having kids?" he asked.

"Yeah, of course I do. I want a big family, but a small wedding though; just me, his family, my family... nothing major and drawn out, because that money can be spent on building my dream home."

Christian

I loved the way she thought, the way she took her time to respond, the way she budgeted her money, the way she valued a dollar, the way she prayed over her food before she ate it and the thoughtfulness she displayed. At the airport she kept trying to take care of things. I could tell she never really had a man to cater to her every need. She was not damaged goods; her heart had never been broken so she was not bitter. She was a woman; a strong beautiful woman.

I used to wonder was it my fault that Miranda and I did not work out, but now I understand it was for a reason; she was not the woman for me. I'm thankful that I didn't settle and marry her, especially since my family did not believe in divorce. I was always taught to work out your problems, and Lord knows I did not want to be stuck in an unhappy marriage the rest of my life.

Even the way this woman slept was peaceful. I wanted to know her flaws, what made her tick and what made her smile. It was our second day here and tomorrow we would be leaving. After our very long walk on the beach, baby girl was knocked out before I could even get her to bed good. Here it is 9 a.m. and she's still sleeping peacefully. She was so beautiful; I could get used to waking up to her beautiful smile.

I wondered if she knew that I killed people for lying to me, or that I supplied the entire East and West coast with heroin, cocaine and pills, would she still let me hold her tight and show her the world? On the way to the hotel, her eyes lit up as she talked about the difference she wanted to make in the world. She had big dreams and desperately wanted to change the community she grew up in. Her passion was for young girls who didn't know who they were. She wanted to mentor kids whose parents were incarcerated or addicted to drugs. A part of me wanted to tell her then, to get out of the car and run; run from me because we were different. Yes, we both struggled to get to where we were now, but I was a hustler. It was in my blood.

I didn't get my hands dirty anymore, however. I didn't even touch or see the work; my trusted commanders handled day-to-day activities such as distribution. Gone were my days of riding dirty, dropping off packages and picking up duffle bags of hundreds. I didn't even carry cash unless I was headed to fuck up the mall or the casino. It took me a long time to reap the benefits of my success, but years later I was the Head Honcho, The Don, the Kingpin, The Connect.

I kissed her forehead, her nose and her lips before making my way down to her bosom, when she began to stir in her sleep. I raised her nightshirt, and my lips found her nipple. I licked slowly, trying to contain the beast inside of me, while I used my other hand to gently massage her thigh and then, "mmm..." a moan escaped between her lips, which ushered me to continue my tasting. Before I knew it, her legs were on my shoulders and breakfast for the day was being served, all-you-can-eat style. I licked, bit, pulled, teased and demolished that pussy.

Just when she thought she couldn't cum any more, I gently stuck two fingers in her pussy and licked, and stroked her gently, humming a love song so she could feel my tonsils on her clit. "Ssssss....shit, Christian stop, please." It looked as if she were rising from the dead. She tried to run but I was going to have her submit to me one way or the other, so I tricked her into thinking it was over. When she turned over to catch her breath, I began placing kisses all over her ass cheeks; I bit into them, smacked her ass and forced her to twerk all over my face. "Hold on to the headboard, and if you let go, I'm going to spank you," I told her.

She nodded and moaned at the same time. I sat her on my face and ate more, and more, and more. Her sweet nectar leaked from her body onto my tongue. Why did she taste so good? Why was her moans so electrifying? I was nutting my damn self without even penetrating her. Please don't let this girl become my drug of choice.

I spanked her ass. "You letting up?" I asked her, as I bit her clit gently. "Owww, no baby I'm not," she whined.

"I'm done anyway; go wash up so we can go shopping." I let her down onto the floor and she fell instantly. "Girl get up, you're alright." I had worn my lil' baby out; I laughed as I wiped my face.

"I'm not, for real. Let's just stay here and watch movies," she pleaded.

"Nope, I want to take you shopping. Come on, baby, come wash my face for me." I picked her up and we shared a shower together.

I slid on some basketball shorts and a white tee, while she donned a khaki and pink romper with pink Old Navy sandals. The first place we were going was to a shoe store.

"Get whatever you want, boo," I told her as I kissed her cheek.

"As long you let me buy you dinner tonight," she said in a serious tone.

"Okay Ms. Independent, dinner on you tonight. I'm ordering an expensive bottle of Henn and the biggest steak they got," I joked.

"That's cool, boo."

"Farren, I want you to get some sandals to match your romper."

"I like my sandals," she hissed.

"I know, but you have the sexiest feet ever; just get you some nice slides ma," I hugged her waist.

"You must really want me to spend your money," she said.

"Don't look at it like that; we're on vacation, just enjoy yourself," I told her.

"Okay," she responded. An hour later she met me in the fragrances section, with a few bags and my receipt that totaled four-thousand, two-hundred dollars. "I love shoes and there were a few of them I've been wanting," she smirked.

"It's cool, baby. These are some of my favorite smells, I just wanted to make sure you liked them before I got 'em" I said to her.

"Did your ex-girlfriend used to wear these?" she asked.

"Yep, and the girl before her and the girl before her; I just like the way it smells on a woman," I told her matter-of-factly.

"In that case, 'ma'am I'll just take a large bottle of Chance by Chanel," she told the attendee at the counter.

"You're something else, ma."

"I'm me, don't place me in a box," she stuck her tongue out.

"Come on, this mall has a lot of nice stores," I told her. The remainder of the day went great. We got matching Fendi sneakers, and I even copped shorty some diamond earrings and a nice Celine bag. She asked could she get her sister something which led to me getting my mom and sisters' gifts as well. By the time we left the Tory Burch store, the leading ladies in each of our lives had purchases from Tory Burch.

"Thanks for dinner," I told her as we prepared for bed. "You're welcome. Thanks for today." She stood on her tiptoes and kissed me; I reached in for another kiss, and another kiss.

"Goodnight," she pulled away.

She just kept doing that. I wasn't pressed for pussy nor was I expecting any from her, but I still wanted to know what was up.

She was in bed with her glasses on, hair pulled in a bun, reading a novel. "Are you a virgin?" I came out and asked her.

"No I'm not, any more questions?" she asked.

"When was the last time you had sex?" I asked.

"I honestly can't remember; two, maybe three years ago," she answered.

"Are you serious?" I asked.

"Very serious," she stated. She had now taken her glasses off, prepared to answer any of my questions.

"But why, what's wrong?"

"I'm focused. Sex causes distraction and it comes with too many emotions. I don't have time for all that."

"When was your last relationship?"

"In college five years ago; I've dated, but nothing more than that."

"Have you ever been in love?"

"Once... he's dead now," she said, never breaking eye contact with me.

"How did he die?"

"His partner killed him right in front of me."

"When was this?" I asked.

"Five years ago."

"But why did he do that?" Curiosity was getting to me.

"Jealousy will get you killed in these streets. He was the man, and his homeboy felt like he owed him something,"

"Who was he?" he asked.

"They called him Dice. He was older; you probably know him, I'm sure."

Did I know him? Hell yeah I knew him; anybody staying in Philly knew him. That nigga ran the city before I took over, but now wasn't the time to tell her I bought all Dice's work from the niggas that robbed him, once he died.

"You were Dice's old lady?"

"Yep, all through high school and college; I was in love," she smiled.

"So he's the only person you've ever been with?"

"Yes. He told me he was a real nigga, and if I didn't get the same feeling I got when I was with him then they weren't real. I ended up having casual sex with this guy; he started wanting more and I pulled back."

"I would have never thought," I mumbled.

"I didn't know things were so complicated back then," she said.

"What do you mean?"

"He was married, had kids, and all of that, but Dice was with me every day. As soon as I graduated, I spent every second and hour with him when I wasn't at school. He put me through school, got me my condo and everything. My BMW was the last thing I bought with his money. His wife tried to act like I was nothing, but she knew I was everything to him," she said, wiping back a tear.

"Damn, shorty."

"It's okay. It matured me. I went through college never working, spending his money and not saving a dime. When he died I was like what do I do now? I've been working ever since. My heart isn't cold towards love, it's just most dudes that try to talk to me are in the streets and I'm done with that lifestyle," she said.

"So what if I was in the streets, then what?"

"Are you?"

"To a certain extent; I have legit businesses though, and nothing will ever happen to you."

"I would have to think about it."

"Are you over him?"

She nodded her head, "Yes. I don't bring him up and I don't discuss him with anyone. His partners still show love in the club, but people die and people move on. I'm okay now."

"I can really see us together," I told her.

"I can too, but I don't play games. The first minute I'm not happy, I'm done."

"See that's not how it goes. We handle that shit and make it work; if you with me, you with me," I told her.

"Well good thing we're still friends right now." She cut the light off and dived under the covers. I went to the patio and rolled a fresh one up. *She used to date Dice.... a fucking kingpin. I* still want her lil' ass, though; she was all that and so much more to me.

Our trip was beautiful and I really enjoyed myself. Farren was so fun to be around. There were times when I had to remember I had just met her, because the way we vibed was nothing I had ever experienced with another female. Farren was real cool and laid back. She was open to trying all the new foods and drinks, and didn't shriek or scream when we held snakes or I asked her to jump off of an eighty-feet cliff with me; she smirked her lips and beat me to it.

"I don't want this trip to end," she whined the next morning as we packed our stuff up.

"This was the perfect getaway for me", I told her.

"Me, too: I can't thank you enough."

"No need, I just wanted to put a smile on your face."

She walked over to me, held my waist and kissed my lips. "That you did, Mr. Knight," she said. I kissed her back, holding her lip with my teeth. She smelled and looked so good.

Farren was becoming my favorite hobby.

The flight back home went smooth and without any turbulence. I texted Greg as soon as we landed to tell him I needed updates on everything that I may have missed while I was out of the country.

"If I say I want you to stay with me tonight, are you gonna call me clingy?" I asked once we landed in Philadelphia and I was taking her back to her car that was parked at my house.

"No, but can we stay at my house because I have to work in the a.m. and I'm desperate for a home cooked meal."

"I can order something to eat," I told her.

"Nah baby, I wanna cook; mashed potatoes, greens, all that," she said, rubbing her stomach.

"You can cook?" That was another brownie point for her.

"Hell yes, why do you think I live in the gym," she joked.

"Well cook your man a meal and I'll be over there as soon as I check on a few things." I fished through my pockets and peeled off two hundred-dollar bills and handed them to her.

"My man? Since when, honey"

"Stop playing with me, sweetie. Call me when it's done. I gotta jet." I kissed her cheek and pulled off. It was officially back to business for me.

"To what do I owe this call," I answered the private number, already knowing who it was.

"Christian Knight, how was your trip my friend?" The person on the other line asked. I didn't like when people watched me or beat around the bush. "How can I help you?" "Stay out of the streets," the person stated firmly before the line disconnected.

Damn, was I doing too much? No one knew who I was, so what made him say that, I thought to myself.

I took my position as "The Connect" very serious. It took a lot of grinding and working my way up from the bottom to the top, to get to where I was. So if that was a warning, I was going to take it serious and get low.

My other phone rang and it was Greg. "Yo where you at?" he asked.

I didn't hesitate to tell him. "Handle the meeting for me; I'll get with you later," I stated.

"You're missing another meeting?" Greg asked, not in a questioning tone but as a concerned friend. Now wasn't the time for me to remind him that I was the connect and he worked for me, so I ignored his question.

"You got it, I'mma holler at you blood," and hung the phone up.

I headed to Farren's house. "You went to the grocery store yet?" I asked her once I had got her on the phone.

"No, I came to put my stuff in the house."

"I'm on the way, just come down and we can go together."

"Okay, boo."

Hours later, we were full and I was high. We were wrapped up under a blanket that her great-grandmother made for her, looking at the television screen watching us. It was obvious our minds were elsewhere.

"What's on your mind?" I asked her, as I ran my fingers slowly through her scalp.

"Everything," she said.

"Talk to me," I replied, as I grazed her belly while her head rested in my lap. I dipped my blunt in the ashtray.

"I don't want to be stressed out; I want to enjoy life," she said.

"All that will come, just stay down and handle your business, bae," I told her. I could have *easily* handled her schooling for her. She could have quit her jobs and focused solely on school. But she was struggling and honestly, she needed to struggle because she didn't need her career handed to her. People who don't work hard don't appreciate anything in life.

"I know. How was dinner? Did you like it?" she asked.

"Hell yeah. You did your thing, boo."

She reached up and kissed me. "That weed taste," she frowned her nose up.

"I'm sorry ma." I ignored her complaint and kissed her back more hungrily than before.

"Let me get up in this." I sat her on my lap facing me.

"I wish," she whispered, and began to kiss me on my neck.

"You wish what? I'm not here to hurt you," I told her as I bit my lip; she was taggin' my neck up something serious.

"I believe you," she said. "You ate my pussy so good last night." She began fondling and licking inside of my ear. I reached under her ass, and stuck my finger in her hole. She tried to rise up, but I went further.

"Ride it like you gon' ride my dick," I told her. She closed her eyes, and I flicked harder. "No, look at me," I told her. "Don't make me have to chase you," I stated firmly, pulling my fingers out her honey pot, making her lick each and every one.

Chapter 3

3 Months Later

Farren

"I haven't seen you in forever," my sister shrieked when I sat at the table. My sister had been begging me to have lunch with her. In between school, work and spending as much time with Christian as possible, I've been running around in circles.

"I know Neeki, I've been working," I told her.

"Did you order already?" I asked her.

"No, I was waiting on you," she said, while responding to someone's text. "Girl, did you see that post Ashley put up yesterday?" she asked.

"Girl, I haven't been on Myspace in months. I eat, sleep, work and go to school," I told her.

My sister, Nikita, was twenty-four, two years younger than me and in her last year of nursing school. We were best friends growing up, and then my dad popped up and saw how I was living and quickly changed my life. And when I say MY life, I mean just me only.

My room was decked out and my sister still slept on the pissy mattress we had our whole lives. But I always shared anything my daddy sent me with her, clothes and all. However, it was never enough. It got to the point where she made me feel obligated to do stuff for her. Even though she was the youngest, she started bullying me and making me ask my dad for stuff that she wanted. My mother was fully aware of what she was doing; however, she turned a blind eye. Years of my family being jealous of me and tormenting me verbally whenever they got the chance, turned me bitter. I spoke to my sister and mom on occasion, but it was no secret they weren't my favorite people.

"Mmm hmmm, so when will I meet your new boo to thank him for my gift?" she asked.

"One day soon; he's busy, I'm busy, you work, mama work," I replied.

"You lookin all icy - Prada bag, Prada shades, I see you sis."

"First of all, I been had these shades and thanks, but it's not that big of a deal."

"Does it feel like being with Dice all over again?" she asked.

"What? What does Dice have to do with being with Christian?"

"Dice made sure you were straight, now this new dude whisking you off to some island just 'cause you failed a test. It's like you got a whole new Dice," she stated.

"And I heard he was that nigga. He's Pookie's connect," she added.

"Next subject before I curse your ass out," I told her to her face.

"Why next subject, because it's true?" she challenged me.

"What's true? I'm sorry that I met a nice guy, Neeki. You of all people should be happy for me. I haven't even taken a guy serious since Dice died and you know that," I looked at her.

"But why now, Farren? Did the money Dice left you run out?" she asked. Never have I ever in life seen the venom in her eyes, as I was seeing at this moment. My best friend, Ashley, used to always say, *"Girl your sister is jealous of you,"* and I would always brush it off; even with Dice. He would tease me all the time saying he could fuck Neeki if he wanted to, and now looking at my blood, I'm seeing that she isn't happy for me.

"I don't know why you and everybody else think Dice left me a whole bunch of money and for the millionth fuckin time, his death was unexpected and he didn't have a will. What little money he did leave me put your ass through nursing school, and got me, you and mama a car, and don't ever forget it, BITCH!" I got up and threw a stack of hundreds on the table.

"Christian said lunch and shopping on him, but you enjoy this by yourself." I grabbed my bag, shades and the keys to HIS Range and dipped.

I went home in a rage. I gathered every little thing he'd bought me in the last three months and found my way to the barbershop where I knew he hung out on Friday afternoons. I texted his phone, "Come outside."

He called instead of replying. "Shopping over already?" he asked. His tone was so deep, Jesus.

"Mmm hmm, come outside," I told him and hung up.

His Caesar cut was fresh and crisp and he donned Burberry tea and khaki cargos. "Sup lady." He opened the driver door and attempted to pull me into him, but I jerked back.

"What's up?" he asked.

"Here are your keys. Can I get my car back?"

He looked at me, but my vintage tint shades hid any emotion. "I didn't get a chance to hit the carwash yet, I been playing cards," he told me.

"That's cool." I cut the truck off and hopped out.

"I'll get up with you later. Where are my keys?" I asked with attitude. "In the office." He was still trying to figure out what the hell was going on and I didn't give him a chance to. I went to retrieve my own keys.

I walked in the shop and didn't speak to anyone. My hair was naturally curly and today I wore it out, all over my face. I had on the cutest little satin shorts and a white cami with my Chanel sandals. They were last season, but I still loved them.

"Yo, what's up with you?" he asked as he closed the door to his office.

"Nothing, where are my keys?" I tossed paperwork all over the place.

"Hey calm down, they're right there." He pointed to a bookshelf.

"Thanks," I replied and prepared to leave.

"What's with all the stuff in the truck? They didn't give y'all shopping bags," he smiled.

"I'm not a charity case; I don't need you buying me shit. I'm with you because I like you, not your money," I yelled.

"Farren, did I I ever say that? Did I ever accuse you of being with me for money?" he asked, as he leaned on his desk.

"I'm just letting you know, I don't need you for anything. You don't have to take care of me. I don't want your partners thinking I'm some broke bitch," I told him.

"I don't care what anyone thinks, because I make my own money so how I choose to spend it is my business. What's up baby, talk to me." He was always so calm; never cursing, never yelling.

"I gotta get out of here," I panicked.

"Give me a kiss first," he said.

"No, just call me later," I told him backing up.

"No. I haven't seen you in two days; come hug me and kiss me Farren, don't leave with an attitude," he paced with me.

I gave in and kissed and hugged him. "We're good, baby. Let me finish up here; here are my keys. The address is in the truck already, just press home. I'mma get your car washed; stop and get us a bottle and cook dinner. I want steak and chicken," he said before smacking me on the butt.

I looked at him and wondered how the fuck did he take my attitude away. I must have been staring. "Baby, you heard me right?" he asked.

I nodded my head. "So come on," he said as he walked me out of the shop and to his car. "You need something?" he asked.

I shouldn't have tried to flex on my sister like that, knowing damn well I could have paid my bills with that money. I hated to tell him I was waiting on my check. "Yeah, to get the groceries," I told him.

He handed me his card, and brushed the hair out of my face. "I like this," he fussed with my hair. "It will be pressed by the time you get to the house," I told him.

"No, don't; I love this wild exotic look on you, Farren." He was so blushing over me. He had to think I was crazy. Less than five minutes ago, I had basically said fuck you, I'm done.

"Are we going to talk about what just happened? I need to talk to you," I told him.

He dashed his tongue into my mouth. "Yes, after you feed me dinner and dessert, we can talk about whatever you want, bae." I kissed him back. His open affection left me speechless sometimes. All I could do was wave and start the car up.

Less than three hours later, I was bathed and in a cami and short set from Victoria Secret. I prepared a feast for him since this just may be the last time we have dinner together. I made him come to my house instead of us going to his. I loved being at my house; it was my safe haven. Over rice pilaf, baked chicken was served with strips of premium sirloin and sautéed veggies. I baked homemade chocolate cookies, enough for him to take to his office for his staff.

My phone vibrated twice. The first text was from Neeki. "Love you!" I didn't respond. The next text was from Christian. "Open the door." In my face were a dozen long-stemmed, yellow roses, my favorite color.

"How did you know?" I asked.

He kissed my forehead, nose and lips. "Know what?"

"My favorite color was yellow."

"On our first date at the Waffle House."

I laughed. "That was not a date, nigga."

"Yes it was. I'm hungry," he complained.

"You look high. You don't wanna bathe first?" I asked.

He looked at me. "No, fix my plate boo. I'm tryna catch the last two quarters of the game."

Little did Mr. Controlling know, his plate was already made. In less than three minutes, he was eating, drinking a beer and talking cash shit to the television because I was too busy cleaning the kitchen and trying to get today's conversation with my sister off of my mind.

"Baby, come here. I'll do those dishes before I leave in the morning," he shouted over the television.

"Who said you were spending the night?" I yelled back.

"Bring that ass here," he replied.

I finished wiping down the counter, and joined him in the living room. "Come here baby,

I miss you," he whispered in my ear as I sat between his arms.

"Missed you more," I told him.

"Thanks for dinner," he said as he massaged my shoulders.

"You're welcome, baby. Is your team winning?" I asked him. I loved a man who was into sports. There was something so sexy about watching him be all into the games.

"You already know," he tickled me. I scanned Myspace while he finished up the game.

"You wanna talk about earlier?" he asked.

"Yes I do," I told him, matter-of-factly.

"Boy, you don't beat around the bush at all!" he joked.

"I'm grown, honey," I told him.

"Shut up. That's your favorite line, *I'm grown,*" he laughed.

"So my sister and I went to lunch earlier, you know, I already told you that part; and before I could even order me a drink, she says, when are we going to meet him, then she said something about you being "The Connect". So I say you know he's busy, I'm busy, you and mommy are busy, we will get to that. So then she says, do you feel like you're with Dice all over again, and I'm like what? Where did that come from? What does Dice have to do with Christian? So long story made short, she feels that I'm getting babied and spoiled all over again. Before I popped her ass I just threw the money you gave me on the counter, called her a bitch and left," I exhaled.

He didn't say anything at first... really for a few minutes. He just smoked. "Do you think your sister may be a little jealous of you?" he asked.

"People used to say that all the time, but that's my sister. I never wanted to believe that because what I have is hers," I told him.

"I'm not spoiling you; I work hard for my money. Anything I give you is because I want to, so you never have to return it. Don't do that anymore," he told me.

I sat up and looked at him. "Christian, you're the same nigga that returned all of your fiancé's shoes. Get out of here with that bullshit," I said.

"I did that because she was unfaithful, so I had reason to," he replied.

"If you say so. Like I tell you all the time, I don't need you for anything - I want that to be clear."

"Farren, okay, who are you trying to convince, me or you?" he asked.

"I'm not trying to convince you or anyone else. No one will ever be able to say I'm with you for anything. I take care of myself; I've been doing it," I hissed.

He wasn't the one I should be angry with. I don't even know why I'm tripping.

"Who hurt you?" he asked me. I just stared back at him. "No seriously, are you scorned? Are you secretly bitter? I asked you were you heart broken, and you said no. I would think after damn near five years of basically being alone, you would be happy to have someone who likes you for you. I'm not tryna just fuck, I'm not asking you to cook dope, and I haven't even pressed you for no pussy. All I ask is for your time and every now and then, cook a nigga a meal," he spoke.

"I'm good, and my heart isn't broken. I knew he was going to die; I didn't know the time or the place, but I know nothing good lasts forever. My hopes were never up, I was just enjoying each day as it came," I replied truthfully.

He shook his head. "That's a fucked up way to live life, not expecting anything. What are you living for then?" he asked.

"I'm just trying to make it," I told him.

"Why didn't Dice's partner kill you?" he came out of nowhere and asked. I figured he heard the rumors that I was fuckin' around with his partner. Many people never knew I was there the night of the murder.

"He didn't see me. I was in the other room changing, and when I was about to walk out of the room to greet his friend, he shot him. I ran to Dice and asked did he want me to call the cops or call someone, but he shook his head no and said he had done too much wrong; they were going to haul him to jail right after he recovered because the place was filled with drugs and guns."

"He had you in a trap?" he asked. I shot him a look like "nigga what you wanna say."

"I'll never have you around that shit." He shook his head.

"Do your parents know what you do?" I asked.

"We on you right now, shorty; finish the story."

"Anyways, he told me he loved me and where to pick up money from. I promised him I would finish school and he told me never settle for a lame ass nigga, and if a nigga didn't make me feel like he made me felt, he wasn't worthy of my time… then he died. I panicked and left the house with a gun, and the money that was in his pocket, and I ran all the way home." That night was crazy. I remembered it like it was yesterday.

1980 - In the Hood of Philadelphia

I couldn't find my house key because by then, I was staying with Dice every day after school; I never came home. I knocked profusely. "Who the fuck is at the door?" my mother hissed.

"It's me mama, let me in," I cried. My hands were filled with blood and so were my clothes.

"Farren, girl what happened to you? Where is -"

"Don't say his name please, don't say his name!" I shut her up. I limped to the bathroom, closed the door, peeled my clothes off and sat in the tub and cried for what seemed like hours. My mother and sister kept knocking at the door. I let my phone go dead because I was unprepared to talk to anyone. I had just lost the love of my life.

"Farren, do you want something to eat?" my mother asked me days later; I didn't respond. Every day was harder and harder for me to process my thoughts. I gave up on school, my line sisters came over every day and checked on me, Dice's homeboys bought money and flowers; none of that mattered to me, I just wanted my man back.

"We're about to head to the funeral," my sister spoke. I knew she was hurting too, but I just couldn't comfort anyone because I was damn sure trying to hold myself up.

I turned my head to the window, and as soon as I heard the door lock, I released tears once again. I remember the first night he told me he loved me; I was like seventeen. Dice was way older than me - wayyyy older, and everyone got onto my mother saying it wasn't right. She approved of me messing with an older man, but my mother knew I was a virgin. She knew she raised me to make the right decisions.

"How was school?" Dice asked me when he picked me up from the curb.

"It was cool until your wife's cousin threw some damn juice in my face. Dice I'm not with this, I'm just not," I yelled.

"Keep calm baby. She crazy, but she ain't that damn crazy. You hungry? You want something to eat?" he asked sincerely.

"Just take me home, please?" I asked.

"Okay baby, whatever you want." He hesitated before he pulled off, but minutes later we pulled up to my projects; my hood, where I was born and raised. "I love you, Farren," he told me.

"No you don't, stop lying," I told him. I was still mad about what happened earlier at school. Dice made it no secret that he was kickin' it with me and he didn't give a fuck what anyone thought. I didn't either, but still it was like I don't appreciate your wife sending people to bully me.

"I do baby. You mean so much to me Farren; you're my best friend," he looked me in my eyes.

"You're mines too; get at me later," I told him and hopped out the car.

He texted me as soon as I made it to my apartment unit. "Why you so nonchalant man, I hate that shit!"

I laughed. I knew he wanted me to say I love you back, but over my dead body. "Get over it nigga. I'm cooking later, I'll put you a plate up."

I snapped out of my daydream to see my sister calling. "Girl, it's packed down here, you need to hurry up." I said okay and hung up. I never had any plans to attend the funeral. I spent six long years with Dice that were filled with love and happiness; there was no need for me to see him like that. I knew he was resting peacefully.

I hated thinking about that painful day. I was convinced I would never love again, but look at God and how he brought Christian to me.

"I'm open to love, but at the same time I want someone on my level," I told Christian.

"What you mean baby?" he asked.

"You have more than me. I don't know anything about you, yet you're always asking me questions. I want someone who is grinding just like I am to get to the top."

"I'm already at the top, boo. I worked hard, I put my time in, I did my dirt, and I fucked hoes. I'm an old man living in my prime right now. I want you to trust me. You should be happy that I'm stable, so if you ever need something I got you. You don't want no broke nigga, ma," he smirked.

"Stop fighting this... stop fighting me. Fuck what your sister talking about; I'm not that nigga Dice. I'm my own man and I like you. By no means am I soft, but I like everything about you; when you're studying, when we go running in the a.m., even when you're sleeping and slobbing, you're beautiful. Don't push me away," he told me.

This man had brought me to tears. Who sent him to me? His parents get a round of applause for raising him so well. He was amazing and literally everything I always hoped for in a man, once I was ready for one. I loved how he took control but still gave me room to make my own decisions. I didn't give a damn what no one thought about me or the reasons I was with him, I know how he made me feel and I know how I made him feel when we were together. And these feelings didn't come from sex, just pure time and attention, something this generation lacks!

I woke up to his phone ringing, but he was knocked out. I silenced it and laid back down in his lap. It rang again and again, and for some reason, I answered it. "Hello," I croaked.

"Hello, who is this?" a female's voice responded.

"A friend of Christian's."

"Can you please give Christian the phone, this is a family emergency," the lady on the phone said.

"Yes, let me wake him up, hold on." I instantly prayed everything was okay.

I shook him gently. "Baby...bae, wake up," I whispered.

He stirred in his sleep. "What's wrong?" He looked alarmed once I handed him the phone. I shrugged my shoulders. As soon he placed the phone to his ear, and said "it's me," it seemed as if the lady on the phone had lost it. Christian rubbed his face over his hands as tears poured out of his eyes. He immediately started looking for his shoes and keys.

"Drive me," he mouthed. I nodded my head and threw on a PINK jumpsuit and sandals. It was the middle of May, but I didn't care. He needed me.

In the car, he never removed the phone from his ear; he just pointed, and made signals for which direction to take. We pulled up to River Oaks Hospital. "I'm on the way up," he told whoever was on the phone before he hung up.

"I'll come back and get you," I told him.

"My dad just had a stroke," he exhaled.

"Is he going to be okay?" I asked.

"I'm not really sure. My sisters all are very, very dramatic. I just hope this one time, they're over exaggerating and he will be home soon," he said.

"I'm here if you need me," I told him.

"Well come in with me. What time do you have to be at work?" he asked. Even in the midst of everything he's faced with, he's still concerned with my well-being. "Don't worry about me, I'll leave an hour before," I told him.

We held hands as we entered the hospital. His family genes were very strong. I instantly spotted his mother, two sisters, and their children. I felt like I already knew them because Christian speaks so highly of them all the time.

His niece quickly ran to his side. "Hi baby girl," he kissed her cheek.

"Mommy said papa's going to die." She burst out in tears.

"Courtney, why would you tell her that?" Christian barked.

"That little girl is so grown; she was all in my conversation. Christian, don't come in here yellin' at me," she said, wiping tears from her face.

I went to sit next to his mother who looked as if she had just lost her world. I knew too well how that felt. "Are you okay?" I asked.

She looked up and smiled. "You're Farrah?" she asked.

I smiled back. "It's Farren; but yes ma'am, that's me." She took my hand in hers. "Time is the one thing that we can't get back in life," she said through tears. Rings aligned her fingers which lay in smooth cocoa skin. For her to be in her sixties, she didn't look a day over forty.

"Everything is going to be just fine," I reassured her. Christian came over and kissed his mother's cheek. "How are you lady?" he asked.

"I'm just here, Christian. I don't know how I am," she wept.

"Daddy is a strong man, what happened?"

"I don't know. I was downstairs cleaning the kitchen and he told me to bring him some water, but I was being stubborn because he had just been downstairs; he could have gotten his own water. So I took my time going up; when I got up there, he was on the floor." She closed her eyes and buckets of tears came out.

"It's okay, let's just wait and see what the doctor says." It wasn't until 6:32 a.m. when a doctor finally came out. "The Knight family?" he asked. We all stood to our feet. "Mr. Knight is most definitely a fighter; he's going to be okay. Let's cut back on the pork and sodium, and no more alcohol. As soon as he's sent to the recovery room, you all can go in and see him; he's up and talking."

The family looked so relieved. I cried tears of joy with them as Christian kissed my forehead. "I'll watch the kids while y'all go back," I told the family. The children had fallen asleep hours ago.

"Thanks Farren...thanks Farren."

"When I come back, I'mma get you home so you'll have time to take a quick nap," Christian said as he kissed me on the cheek.

After reviewing some key words for a quiz I had tonight, I scrolled through my text messages. I barely responded to people. I just didn't have the desire to.

"Farren, what are you doing here girl?" my sister approached me.

I was too tired to even go off on her for yesterday's activities. "Christian's dad had a mild stroke," I told her, barely looking up.

"Awww, is he okay? I'm sorry to hear that," she said.

"Yes, he will be," I told her.

"You ready, bae?" Christian's voice came down the hallway.

"Yes, if you are," I told him. Just looking over at my eye candy made me moist, and I knew this was the wrong time, but his skin the color of a melted Twix bar, his perfect teeth, wide smile and dimples, always made me warm on the inside.

"This is my sister, Neeki; Neeki, Christian," I said dryly.

"We've been eager to meet you," she said giving him a hug.

"Aww, really? We will have to do something when Farren gets done with finals." He was so calm and collected.

"Let's go," I told him. He hugged and kissed his sisters. His mother agreed to stay at the hospital with her husband, and I don't blame her because I would have done the same thing.

Chapter 4

Christian

July 4th weekend came so fast. This has
been such a nice summer; business was
booming, new contracts were coming in by the
load, and Farren passed her classes. I knew she
could do it. She had three months to tighten up
because August would be here before we knew
it. We decided to have a barbeque for close
friends and family at the house. I still don't
know why she didn't just move in. We had been
conversing for seven months and she still
insisted on getting out of bed and going to her
house some nights.

"Baby, can I cut the oven off?" I yelled
upstairs.

Farren did a great job cooking everything. Little did she know, my sisters were unsure of her cooking and they were still going to bring their own food. My mother fell in love with Farren and my niece is always over whenever Farren doesn't have to work.

My sisters liked her too, but they were still skeptical due to Miranda. I was grown; I didn't give a damn how they felt. I didn't get to pick their husbands for them, and I still paid for each of their weddings. All my partners would be here soon, along with Farren's line sisters, and her mother and sister would be coming over for the first time.

"Yes boo," she said. My dick got hard when I saw her. "Damn ma," I told her. She put her hands on her hips. "Chris, I can have on a dirty tee-shirt and you still gon' say, damn ma," she laughed.

I didn't care what she thought; she was always looking pretty to me. I loved her style.

She had so much flavor. Today she donned a long tangerine dress, the back completely out, and her rose gold Rolex with the earrings to match, that I brought her for passing her classes. My baby was looking too fly.

"I'm getting some of that pussy tonight!" I smacked her ass.

"You might," she joked back. Unfortunately I still haven't broken her back, but I stopped tripping because we spent quality time together and I enjoyed every minute I was in her presence.

The doorbell rang before I could give her smart ass a reply. "Hi son," my mother spoke gently as my daddy walked in with a cane. "What's up daddy," I felt him on the back. He nodded his head. "I wanna sit down," he said. "Yes sir, come in here." I led him to the living room, before asking my mom, "How is he doing?" Once we made it to the kitchen, all of my family had arrived. This was going to be a joyous weekend.

"He's stubborn, but he's fine. I let him sip my wine last night," mama laughed. Chloe's face turned beet red. She was daddy's pride and joy. "Don't do that again," she hissed. "That's my husband child, mind your business," she fanned her off. I decided to deal with mama later.

"Yooooo!" Greg, my best friend from back then came in, followed by Jeremiah, my partner and right hand man.

"Hi Greg," Courtney smiled. No one could tell me that Greg and Courtney didn't mess around when we were younger, but that wasn't my business.

"Everyone, this is my mother, Nakia and my sister, Nikita," Farren smiled.

My mother said, "It's a pleasure to meet you, you have a wonderful daughter." Her mother smiled back. "Come on, let me show y'all the house," Farren said.

"She's definitely the outcast," Chloe mumbled.

Greg laughed and said, "I was thinking the same thing."

I didn't know what they meant and I wasn't about to entertain it. I went to meet my future mother-in-law. "Hi Ms. Nakia, it's so nice to finally meet you." I kissed her on her cheek and squeezed Nikita's shoulder.

"This is a big, nice house. Thank you for letting us come over," she said.

"Anytime," I told her. Farren looked at me and smiled.

"Can I get y'all anything?" I asked.

"No we're fine, we're just going to catch up with Farren. We barely see her now," her sister spat.

After I ignored her completely, I looked at Farren and she nodded, so I went to enjoy my family. The day turned into night and before you knew it, Farren's family had gone and left.

"I'm sorry about that everybody," she apologized as soon as she walked into the family room.

"Girl I understand. I hate going to my husband's parents' house because they act so funny," Courtney told her.

"What's wrong with your sister" Chloe asked.

Farren shook her head. "I don't really know. Ever since I got with Christian her nose has been turned up. I kept asking her did she want to come in here with y'all, especially being that you're a doctor and that's what she eventually wants to do, and she kept saying no." Farren looked defeated, but at least she tried and that was all that mattered.

"Do you all have different fathers?" my mother asked.

"Yes ma'am; I'm sure you all can tell the difference."

Greg shouted, "hell yeah!" I looked at him. Farren was high yellow and honey golden, but her mother and sister were dark as tar. Farren spoke well, and her mother and sister seemed to act as if they had never been anywhere; well her mother seemed reserved.

"I spent a lot of time with my daddy growing up. He's an attorney out in California, living with his white wife which should explain the difference," Farren told everyone. That shocked me, too. I always assumed she didn't have a daddy.

"How often do you visit him?" my nosey ass sister asked.

"I work a lot, plus with school, it's been a minute I'm embarrassed to say. We text a lot, though," she said.

"Girl, I thank God for my brother every day. I don't see how people work and go to school," Chloe said.

Farren shook her head. "I'm making it." The night was full of pleasantries as we ate, drank, played games, and watched movies.

My family hugged me and Farren goodnight. "Baby come to bed, I'll have a cleaning service handle all that." She was always ready to clean, but we had a long weekend. I just wanted to wash her and put her to sleep.

After our shower together, we lay in bed with a few candles lit, and held each other naked. "Let's go get tattoos in the morning," she said. "Tattoos of what?" I asked. I personally felt like I was too old to be getting matching tattoos, but I didn't want to hurt her feelings. "I want to get your name and a crown," she said. "Well you do that baby," I kissed her.

"What are you going to get? She asked.

"Nothing. Ink doesn't prove my love for you."

"Love?" she asked.

"You know what I mean."

"You love me?" she asked.

"Not yet, but I have love for you." I kissed her, and held her tight as we let the sounds of Adele lead us to a peaceful sleep.

"Baby!" I jumped up at the sound of Farren's voice.

"What?" I asked. I barely got to sleep like I wanted to, so when I did, I didn't like being woken up. "My car won't start and I'm late for work!" she screamed, jumping up and down. "I don't know why you won't let me get you a car; that shit is through," I told her, pulling the covers back. "Because I've been paying the note too long and I'll feel like I've been wasting my money. I'll get it fixed when I get my next check," she said. I didn't even feel like going there with Miss Independent.

"Why did you wake me up again?" I asked.

"Can I borrow the keys to one of those automobiles in the garage, I'll come right back after work." "You didn't have to ask, and when you get off, I won't be here. I'mma be in new York til' late tonight, finishing the walls on that restaurant so I'll catch you later," I told her, scanning my phones for notifications.

"Well after I get off work, I'mma drop your stuff off at the cleaners, and pick up something to cook. I'll leave your plate in the microwave, 'cause I'm sure I'll be sleep when you get here," she kissed me on the cheek.

"I'm going back to my house tomorrow," she yelled before she went through the garage. Yeah, yeah. I knew if I asked her to stay another night she would say yes. I don't know why she still tried to act so hard; I know she's mine.

It was no point in attempting to go back to sleep. I took a shower and slid on a DG suit, with a teal shirt and black dress shoes. Upon entering the kitchen, the aroma of hot breakfast hit me in the nose, causing me to smile. The girl did the simplest things but they meant the most to me. She left me a twenty dollar bill with a note, "lunch on me," and breakfast in Tupperware.

I texted her once I hit the highway. "Have a beautiful day baby, see you tonight; make alfredo for me, please?" I had grown accustomed to her cooking, and certain dishes I wanted more than once a week such as her alfredo.

I pulled up to a warehouse. I didn't plan on starting my day killing anyone, but business called and I had to answer.

"Morning Boss." There were only a few trusted people who I allowed to be in my presence.

My childhood best friend, Greg, was in the gutter with everybody. He lived, ate and breathed the streets. Greg knew everyone who worked for me by first and last name. He knew where each of their mothers lived, where the baby mother resided, down to where the workers' children got their teeth cleaned. Greg held every person accountable for their work, their actions and most importantly their fuck-ups. He didn't believe in second chances or extensions.

The operation was run tight and excuses were tools of incompetence. This wasn't your ordinary squad or group. This wasn't a gang of niggas selling weed. There was a strict process to joining such an elite group of people. Our clientele included the "Who's Who" of major cities. Grams or ounces weren't even in my vocabulary. I moved real weight by the ton, not even by the pound.

People were placed on a waiting list just to get product. If you didn't reserve your order by a certain time and date, your clients would have to wait. Christian believed in organization. His illegal business was run just as smooth as his legit businesses. All of the money went into the same category, yet different accounts. Loyal people were hard to come by. We worked too hard to climb the ladder of success, and I refused to let a rat be our downfall.

Greg dapped his friend up. "You know this lil' nigga? I think we both fucked his sister a while back".

Christian looked over at the young boy who was beaten to a bloody pulp. "Why would you steal something that wasn't yours?" he asked.

The boy's eyes were swollen shut, and blood profusely leaked out of them. He ignored Christian's question.

He was in a good mood on this morning, so he kneeled in front of him, careful not to get his suit dirty, and asked him again, "Why would you steal something that wasn't yours?"

Either the boy refused to speak or he was unconscious. Whichever way it went, he had to die; he had now seen Christian's face.

"Your mom is good people. I think she used to play Bingo with my Aunt Dorinda," Christian continued.

"Man, fuck you! Kill me and get out of my face," he spat.

"Just because you ignored my question and chose to be rude, you're going to die on your own." Christian stood up and instructed one of the guys to not feed him or give him water. He wanted the young boy to suffer day in and out and think about his stupid ass decision and how it caused him his life.

"I'm out of here. I got meetings to get to," he told Greg.

"Alright. You didn't have to come, though," Greg told him, as he walked Christian back to his car.

"I was in a good mood this morning... gotta ride through every now and then," he told his home boy before he honked the horn and pulled off.

Farren

Work went by fast, and I was more than grateful. I made my way to La Perla, a fancy lingerie store, and purchased something hot and sexy for Christian. I then went to the grocery store, and ran all the errands I promised I would handle for him, and still had an hour to get some cardio in. While dinner cooked, I sipped wine and caught up on some reading. I saw my sister calling and wondered what the hell she wanted. "Hello," I answered.

"What up sis, what you doing tonight?" she asked loudly.

"It's Monday, girl, nothing; I been at work all day," I told her.

"We're going to get drinks tonight. Come out," she said.

"Who is we?" I asked. My sister wasn't one to hang with many. "Tasha, Niecy and them," she said and I frowned. "No ma'am, y'all be safe," I told her.

"Okay cool. Well can you tell whoever bartending tonight that I'm your sister?" I knew then and there she knew I wasn't going, she just didn't wanna be rude and come out and ask me to cover her drinks tonight.

"Mmm hmm," I told her, ready to hang up.

"Okay and I paid mommy's rent this month; it was hard but girl I did it, and it felt good," she said. I'd been paying her rent for years. "That's good girl," I said. She held the phone for a few seconds. "What are you doing tonight?" she asked.

"Washing my hair, doing some Pilates, and catching up on 'Young and the Restless'." I yawned and I was nowhere near tired.

"Girl, you're getting old. Well alright then, talk to you later," she said, and I quickly disconnected the call. Tomorrow I'll ask God to soften my heart, but not tonight.

Dinner was prepared, and I went to shave and prepare for what was going to be a long night. Afterwards, I shimmered my body with Dust by Dior, and twisted my hair in the front. Christian loved my hair in its natural state, and tonight it was all about him. I placed six-inch Louboutin heels on my feet, slid the white thong over my ass and the white bra which snapped in the front. My man loved white it; was his favorite color. I doused a little perfume on; not too much, because my bath already had me smelling good. I haven't talked to Christian all day, and I was missing the hell out of my man.

I went downstairs and sat at the kitchen table, scanning Myspace, and waiting on my man's arrival. I kept yawning; today was really a long day.

Christian

The dash of my car read 4:42am. It was beyond late and I was tired as hell. It seemed as if everything that could go wrong, went wrong today; contractors were late, I had to make a little boy whose sister I grew up with, suffer today, walls measured incorrectly and my shipments were coming in late from the boat. I was one stressed motherfucker. I planned on taking me a week-long vacation as soon as this restaurant was up and running. I don't even know how I made it home; I kept rubbing my eyes and yawning. I thanked God for safe travels the minute the garage door closed.

I walked in the house and my stomach rumbled which reminded me I hadn't eaten since breakfast this morning. I didn't see any pots and pans. I made a left into the dining room and saw a feast prepared for a king; she did all this for me. I popped a piece of chicken in my mouth and came out of my shoes right then and there. I knew baby was sleep; she's always in bed before twelve. I went to the living room to cut the television off, and instantly my dick got hard. Farren looked like a naughty angel in all white lingerie and red lipstick, and the highest heels I had ever seen her wear. I stood over her and just stared look at my baby, man. Damn... tonight must have been my lucky night.

"Baby wake up, daddy's home," I told her. "Nigga please," she yawned.

"What time is it?" she asked.

"Past your bedtime, come on," I told her, as I helped her up and led her to our bed.

"Can you put that food up, please?" she asked, before she fell back asleep. I took her heels off for her, and kissed her forehead.

Damn, she went all out and I came home too late. I knew she had to be up in less than three hours for work, so I let her sleep. I ate dinner, showered, and joined my baby in bed.

When I woke up Farren was already out the door. She had been working so much lately, we would both be in need of a vacation soon.

Today I had to handle more hood duties, and I wasn't impressed. Lately I kept having to step in and check on shit. This is not how I liked to spend my days.

Every time I headed to the hood, the words, "*Stay out the streets*" replayed in my head, and I knew I had to tighten up. "So how are the numbers looking?" I asked one of the lil' niggas. I hated being in the trenches. I'd put my time in years ago and I paid niggas to handle my dirty work; all I wanted to do was collect.

"It's been good, boss." He nodded his head and inserted more money into the machines.

"How is it good and I'm here, Ramone? Whenever you see me, know that it's not good." I didn't threaten him; I simply gave him the heads up by informing him he should never feel joy when seeing my face.

"I feel you," Ramon replied.

"I don't want to come back here or I'm probably going to kill you. Tighten up on your people." I kept it real with him. This was my second time having to straighten a situation out, and I wasn't happy about it at all. I grabbed two duffle bags and headed to my truck, before realizing it was a dumb decision,

"I'm going to have somebody pick that money up in an hour," I told Ramone before leaving.

I planned on surprising my baby for lunch today.

I valet parked my truck; the Range Rover was my favorite vehicle. Out of all the cars I owned, it damn near drove itself sometimes. I walked into Nordstrom's and found my baby carrying out tons of boxes. I saw that she looked flustered and busy, so I browsed around the other departments until I knew her break was near.

"And how may I help you, sir," she approached me with a smile. Her blouse was tucked in her jeans and she was bare - no makeup. I always loved her when she was like this.

"I'm here to take my lady to lunch," I smiled back and hugged her.

"Good, I'm hungry. I didn't eat last night or this morning," she said, pointing her finger in my chest. "Baby, if I'd known all that was going down, I would have been home before you," I told her.

"It's okay; we've both been grinding," she assured me.

"Take off for the rest of the day. I miss you," I told her.

She shook her head. "It's the first of the month. I need all the money I can get; car note, bills, rent, loan payments, membership dues for delta, I'm helping my mama get her credit together, your birthday coming up," she rambled.

"Am I your man?" I asked her.

"Yes Christian, you are," she told me.

"So go take off the rest of the day, it's slow in here." I patted her on the butt.

She drove her car back to the house and she changed into shorts and her Burberry burgundy tee, before we went to enjoy lunch at Zenburger. "You're so Hollywood; why do you have those shades on?" I asked her.

"Because you wanted to sit outside and the sun is in my eyes," she told me.

I snapped a picture of her; she was so beautiful to me.

"I miss you," I told her.

"I've been missing you more; you come home so late," she whined.

"You go to bed too early," I told her.

"I have to be at work at 8 every morning," she hissed.

"You can cut your hours whenever you want to," I told her and sipped my Hennessy.

"You contradict yourself a lot," she replied.

"I'm listening."

"First you tell me your fiancé quit her job and sat around doing nothing all day; you now want me to do the same. If I do that then you'll lose respect for me and I won't be your equal," she told me.

"Bae, you think too hard. She did all that on her own. I want you up when I get home, not dog tired and complaining because your feet hurt. I don't want you struggling when you got me." I held her hand and looked in her eyes when I spoke, because my words were real and I didn't compare her to Miranda, ever.

"Okay," she said.

"What else you wanna do today?" I asked.

"As long as I'm with you, I don't care," she smiled.

Miss Independent paid for lunch, of course. We then went and got pedicures and massages, and decided to spend the rest of the day in New York.

"Do you still want to get married... like, are you excited to get married?" Farren asked.

"What you mean?" I asked.

"I'm saying... you and the girl were planning your wedding up until a few weeks ago. Are you like fuck weddings right now?" she questioned.

"I gotta become your boyfriend before I become your husband," I teased.

"I'm not ready for marriage, baby, I'm just asking a question."

"Mmm hmm, come on." I pulled her closer to me. It was the first time for both of us, going to the aquarium and visiting The Apollo Theatre. We stopped in the mall to get undergarments and clothes for dinner tonight. My phone had been on silent all day and when I glanced down, I just happened to see the light. "What up," I answered my second line. I had two iPhones; one for personal and business, and the other, a trap phone.

"Yo, we got hit," this cat named Peanut yelled in the phone.

"What are you telling me for? Handle it," I said before I hung the phone up. Farren ran up to me. "Baby you like these?" she held up some pajama pants.

"Why didn't you pack that outfit from last night?" I asked before I slid my phone in my back pocket.

"Oh, you want me to get something like that?" she looked back at me.

"Yes, ma. Turn up on me tonight," I said, smacking her ass. People in the store looked at us; she didn't care and I damn sure didn't.

We checked in at the Ritz Carlton hotel, dressed and had dinner at Dolce, followed by dessert. Before turning in, we stopped by a bar to get drinks. I rolled up and returned phone calls while Farren bathed and prepared for bed. "Yo, what the fuck I don't understand is why everyone feels comfortable calling me. When shit goes wrong, my number is not the number to call. How are people even getting my number," I questioned Greg.

Farren cleared her voice, and I turned around to see baby girl in nothing but a thong. I made a motion with my finger and she turned around for me. I noticed a tattoo on her hip: my name with a crown. "When you get that?" I mouthed. She mouthed back, "Yesterday." I told her to come out on the balcony where I was already, leaning against the rail. She held me and kissed me all over my face while rubbing my dick between my shorts. "Tonight it's all about you," she whispered and licked in my ear.

"I'mma hit you back," I barely managed to get out before I disconnected the call.

She dropped to her knees, and on the 40th floor for the first time in eight months, I got my dick sucked; it was like nothing I ever received in life. She took her time, knowing when to use her hands, when to suck, lick, pull, bite, hum, slurp, swallow, choke, or deep throat; this blessing was well worth the wait.

"How are you feeling, Daddy?" I looked down at her before answering her question. Farren was playing in her pussy while she put my balls in her mouth.

"Good baby, real good," I whispered. I bit the inside of my mouth as I attempted to hold back moans and grunts. I pulled away and picked her lil' ass, carrying her to the bed. I stuck my finger in her pussy and cream instantly poured out. I removed my clothes and said, "You know I'm about to tear you up, right?" I cut the lights off and found a condom.

"I deserve it," she laughed.

"Damn sure do. Open up them legs and tell me to fuck you," I commanded. I stroked my dick as I met her in the middle of the bed. Farren tensed up when I met her entrance. "Stop," I told her. I kissed her all over her face, nose, lips, and neck, and smothered her breast while making her grind on my fingers. I was gon' have baby girl cumming all night whether she wanted to or not.

"Oooooohhhhhh," she said as I played with her clit a little faster. I removed it instantly and slid my rod into her. She screamed out in pain and I moaned with pleasure.

"Omg, shit baby, this pussy mine," I said as I grinded her back out. I pushed her legs over her shoulders, and took my time making the pussy surrender to daddy; I fondled her breast and played with her clit at the same time. She really didn't know how to react or what to do. I had her paralyzed.

For hours I folded her up, bent her over, and worked every inch of the hotel, as we came back to back together. Our night was more than memorable and I knew then that without the sex, I was feeling her. She had become my everything in a short amount of time, but with the lovemaking I knew we were a match in heaven, and she was destined to be with me.

Farren

"Wake up sleepy head," I whispered to Christian. Baby was snoring lightly, dick out and all. I had to get to work and this drive back to New York would be crazy considering the traffic. "Call out," he whispered and turned over.

"I can't, come on," I pulled at him. "Take the car, I'mma catch a ride," he mumbled.

"Christian, are you serious? Get up," I frowned.

"Give me a minute; gon' and get dressed," he said.

"Dressed? I have to go home and get dressed for work."

"I promise if you call out I won't ask you to call out anymore; just come lay with me," he told me.

I looked at him and I couldn't say no to that pouty face. I know how hard he had been working. Honestly, we both needed this sleep. I made the call and took my clothes off. Once he felt me join him in bed, he rolled over and pulled me closer to him. "Thank you," he kissed my face. "For what?" I asked.

"Last night...and spending another day with me," he kissed me again.

"What happened last night? I don't know what you're talking about," I played lost.

He slowly slid his hand between my legs. "Oh you don't?" he asked. I shook my head, egging him on. The last thing I wanted to do was get addicted to this man's sex, but he was making it so hard.

Before I knew it I had cum multiple times, and he had me bent over the edge of the bed, begging for mercy. He ran his hands through my hair and pulled my head back so he could kiss my spine and fuck me at the same time. "Say it's mine," he commanded.

"It's yours," I whimpered.

"No, spell my name out, slowly," he smacked my ass.

He was literally giving me pain and pleasure, and I couldn't take it. I stopped throwing it back and tried to catch my breath. I attempted to crawl on the bed and under the covers, but he grabbed my leg, flipped me over and picked me up. He cradled me in his arms and stuck nine inches of steel inside of me. It touched my soul. He began bouncing me up and down. "Yeah like that," I told him. "Kiss me," he said. We kissed roughly and I massaged his scalp as he continued to pounce in me. It was like we were having sex in the air, it was so good. We finally came down back to Earth and were spent out on the floor.

Minutes later, I was still attempting to catch my breath while he wiped his face with a towel. "Let's go bathe." He held his hand out to help me up. After our shower, we dressed in yesterday's attire and headed back to our side of town.

"What you gotta do today?" I asked him, as I got off onto the exit to his house. "I'm chilling. I'll hit the gym later and go check on my daddy, why wassup?" he asked as he texted someone back on his cell phone.

"Just asking. I'mma go to my house and do some laundry, and I'mma go to work for a few hours," I told him.

"Okay bae," he said.

We pulled into the garage and he kissed me goodbye. "Why you gotta leave?" he held my hand.

"Because I've been with you three days straight," I giggled.

"What happens when you spend every day with me for the rest of your life?" he asked. I couldn't stop staring at him. Christian meant everything to me, but it was so hard for me to admit it.

"We will cross that bridge when we get there," I told him.

"Alright boo, I'll catch you later," he told me.

He pulled out his wallet and handed me his card. "What's this for Christian?" I asked.

"Spend your check on you, and pay your bills with this. Or you can spend your check on bills and spend this card on you," he told me.

"Why?" I asked. I didn't understand why he insisted on taking care of me, I just didn't.

"Don't question it Farren. I'll holler at you later." He kissed me and basically sat me in my car and closed the door.

Once I got off work and was on the highway, I called my best friend and soror who I missed dearly. She was enjoying her life in Atlanta. "Hey sis!" she answered the phone. We didn't talk everyday but when we did it was always worth it.

"I miss you," I whined.

"I missed you more. How's work been? I need that discount," she yelled. Ashley was the total opposite of me... loud and obnoxious.

"Just tell me what you want sis and I'll mail it to you," I told her.

"How is that fine ass man of yours?" she asked.

"We went to New York for the day. I'm headed back to my house now," I told her.

"New York? Girl we done came a long way from dating drug dealers. Sis, I'm so happy for you. You deserve all of this." I was so happy that I had her in my life. It's not too often we meet genuine people, especially females, that really care about you being happy.

"Ashley, I'm so nervous. I don't want to mess it up," I told her.

"What you mean?" she asked.

"I find myself feeling him; staring at him in his sleep, girl, praying for us. I actually like coming home to him; he's so sweet and attentive. I love cooking for him and cleaning his house. I don't feel worthy, Ashley," I told her. It's not that I was insecure or anything. It was an amazing feeling to have someone like me for me. I loved how we were on the same page about life, love and us.

"How are you not worthy? Why are you not worthy? Farren, you won't drive him away," she got on me. Tears came out of my eyes and I didn't know why. I walked in my house, locked the door and sat on the couch. "I was sixteen years old sleeping with a grown, married man with kids. I thought it was cute. Girl, karma is real," I admitted.

"Farren that was years ago. What does Dice have to do with this?" she asked.

I went back in time and remembered how dumb I used to be. I attempted to wipe the tears as I remembered the day I saw Dice's wife in my hood.

A long time ago

Ashley and I were coming back from the candy lady house and there she was, standing outside of a Porsche in the nicest threads and finest jewelry. "Which one of y'all yellow girls is Farrah?" she spat.

"It's Farren," I spoke up. I was in the 11th grade and wasn't scared of anybody, period. I was

from Hardy Projects. I had been picked on and bullied my whole life. My mama stopped letting me come home crying and she would send me right back out there to handle the shit. People were so jealous of me and I didn't understand why; I mean who wanted to turn red when they cried? I was high yellow with hair that was always fuzzy and curly because my mother could barely afford to send me to the hairdresser. I even hated how big my ass was. I was shy and didn't like all the attention on me.

My mother had me at the age of seventeen; it was a generation curse in my family. Everybody in my family was pregnant before 18 and I made it my business for it not to happen to me. My mama met my daddy at a cleaning job, but he was a high-priced attorney. She claimed they fell in love and was really together. When I was younger I believed he only sent child support to keep my mother quiet and out of his business, but either way it went, my father was always there when it was important; he never missed any of my accomplishments.

"I don't give a damn what your name is bitch," she said.

"Oh okay," I said and I kept walking, with Ashley following suit.

Her cousins all got out the car, and his wife yelled out again, "Lil bitch, where you going?"

"Who are you calling a bitch ma?" I asked in the nicest tone with a smile.

Ashley asked me did I want her to get my sister. "I'm good," I told her.

"Look lil' girl, stay away from my husband. This is your only warning," she said.

I smiled and said, "Okay." I wasn't going to turn my back anymore; hoes from Philly didn't play fair, especially the ones from across the tracks.

I was relieved she bowed down easily because I didn't feel like fighting today; I had been at track practice for the majority of it.

I ran upstairs and asked my cousin could I borrow his car. "Dice will fill it up." I knew that would get his ass, 'cause most likely the mf was on empty.

"Alright cuz, and I want it on full, too," he said and threw me the keys to his Impala.

"Ashley, ride with me," I told her. She shook her head. "Nah, Farren I'm not running up behind that nigga. His wife just came for you," she yelled. She didn't like Dice at all. She thought it was creepy and she didn't tolerate our "relationship" one bit.

"Come on girl and shut up, I'm not stuntin' that hoe," I told her. I had on my track shorts, a Nike shirt and tennis shoes, all complimentary of Dice; he supported my dreams.

I was driving illegally. My mother had been promising to take me to get my license, but until then I didn't give a damn. My whole family stayed in Hardy Projects, so I was forever driving somebody else car.

I pulled up and told Ashley to stay in the car. "Not where the hell we're at; I'm going in," she said, hopping out the car. Before I met Dice I didn't have a cellphone, and he had been promising to get me one for a few weeks. We had only been talking for a month or two, though he had been chasing me for six.

I banged on the door. "Who you looking for lil mama?" some dirty man said, licking his lips. I pushed him out the way, and told Ashley to come on.

Lo and behold, there was the Dominican kingpin himself. Dice was red as they came; short and stout with freckles all over the bridge of his nose, but don't ever get it twisted - he was nothing to play with. He was sitting with a gun on his lap, and one by his foot.

"Why is your wife coming to look for me, and how the fuck does she know where I stay?" I spat. He looked up at me. "Wassup Farren," he said sarcastically.

His partners all looked at me. I'm sure they were thinking who is this young girl, coming in here cutting a fool. It would be five long but crazy years, where they would see me do more than act an ass.

"Answer my question!" I yelled.

He paused the game and stood up. "Why are you fussing? Come in here." He grabbed my arm. "Hey Ashley," he smiled at her. She just took a seat on the couch. Ashley already knew what was up.

He yanked me into the other room and closed the door. "Don't be coming in here like you hot shit, you call first," he told me.

"With what phone?" I asked.

"We gon' handle that tomorrow," he said.

"Your wife and her busted ass cousins were standing outside of my building. Dice I promise you, I'm not with the mess," I clapped my hands.

"How was school?" he ignored me. I hated when he played me like it was nothing.

"Dice, I'm about to clock your ass, straight up," I told him. He pushed on me and kissed my neck. "You be looking so good when you get out of practice," he whispered and held me close to his body.

"Yeah, yeah, whatever! Let me get up out of here," I told him.

"Don't be worried about her crazy ass," he told me. I wasn't stuntin' shit he was saying. He walked me and Ashley to the car, and peeled off a few hundreds. "Go get you a phone tomorrow, and I better be the only nigga textin' you," he *said and kissed me on the cheek. I counted the money once we got to a red light, and handed Ashley a c-note.*

"Girl, take this back," she said.

"No girl, this nigga be giving me so much money. I'mma go get me a celly tomorrow, and get my hair braided for the summer and save the rest so I can take my ACT; Ashley I'm getting out the hood," I told her. "Me too, girl."

We stuck to our promises and graduated top of our class. Ashley and I attended LU and pledged together. I majored in Criminal Justice and she majored in Psychology. At the present, she was enjoying life in Atlanta.

"Girl, Dice is gone. Don't let him keep you from love. I don't see how you've been going all those years without getting any dick," she said.

"You're right; visit me soon," I told her.

"Ain't shit in Philly, you come visit me."
Ashley hated coming home. All of her family was
dead and gone, and we didn't really hang with
any of the girls from our hood.

"I might come for Labor Day," I told her,
and we agreed to talk again next week. I ran a
hot bubble bath and enjoyed a glass of wine,
while reminiscing on the past few months. I was
so happy and that, I couldn't deny. Me and
Christian spent real time together.

I remember the first time we went to the
strip club; it was crazy. I really didn't wanna go.
I was never one of those girls that had to be in
the club.

*It was a few months ago when he asked me
randomly to step out with him one night.*

*"Gon' and get dressed, boo," he patted me on the
butt.*

*"I'll be here when you get back." I was really
enjoying the Lifetime movie I was watching. "No,*

we're going together. You've been studying for midterms and now that they're over, we about to turn up." He took the remote and cut the television off.

I moved like a turtle while Christian rolled up. As I scanned my overnight bags that had piled up at his house over time, I decided on a red Herve Ledger dress I had for years and never wore. Dice brought this dress years ago.

"Expensive taste," Christian complimented.

"It was a gift," I told him. The only thing I'll ever spend my hard earned money on is shoes!

"Let me guess...Dice?" he asked.

I didn't answer. I slid my t-shirt over my body, tied up my red Giuseppe shoes, added a little eyeliner and dabbed some perfume on. "You ready?" I asked him.

"Yep, come on, sexy." I looked over at my sexy ass boo. He donned a button down and jeans

and sneakers; his Rolex glistened. If only I could just give him a glimpse of this good loving.

He handed me stacks of ones and told me to make it rain. We had so much fun that night. I drank a lil' more than a lil' bit. His friends and the ones that did bring significant others, all seemed to enjoy their night in our private VIP section. What I love about Christian is he was a businessman. His entire team was getting money, and they were all college graduates, or so I thought.

"Let me see how you twerk it, ma," he whispered in my ear.

I bent over and touched my toes, and made my ass jiggle; one cheek, then the other one, then both. He smacked my ass, gripped my waist, pulled me to his lap, and I bounced up and down as he exhaled his blunt. "All this ass is mine?" he asked.

"It could be." I turned around and kissed him hungrily in the mouth.

The water turning cold is what brought me out of my daydreaming. I realized I didn't want to be without my man tonight or any more night. With the towel tied lazily around my body, I searched for my phone to call Christian. "Hello... hello," he yelled in the phone.

"Where are you?" I asked with a raised eyebrow.

"At the strip club," he yelled back.

"Which one?"

"Stroker's," he yelled. "Bae, I'mma hit you back," and he disconnected the call. Ain't no way in hell he was about to be all in the club getting drunk, and then going to an empty house. I was going to the strip club to get his key and wait up until he got home.

I searched my closet for something casual, yet cute. I decided on a black slanted skirt, neon BEBE pumps and a silk sheer wife beater. I added my Rolex Christian bought me, and my favorite f21 hoops. I hopped in my ride and pulled up to the club, paying extra to park in the front.

I scanned the club for Christian and I spotted him, Greg, Jeremiah and a few of his other partners making it rain amongst other things. Christian was chilling as always. My man was always the laid back one. I ordered me a Patron and pineapple juice, and made my way towards my boo.

People were stopping me left and right. "Lil' Farren, what you doing in here?" I didn't even look back to see who called my name.

I stepped in the booth. "What up Farren?" "Farren what it do boo?" his partners showed love.

"Look at you." He stood up and turned me around as I blushed. "You like?" "You know I do," he sat me in his lap. "Why are you carrying a gun?" I asked him. For him to be a business man, his having a gun threw me off. "You can never be too careful," he told me. Before I could ask him another question concerning the weapon, my song came on. *"Hold on wait a minute, y'all thought I was finished!"*

I got up and threw money in the club. Before I could turn around to dance for my bae, bullets ran through the club; well I thought I heard bullets, but the music was still playing so it couldn't have been. Then I heard it again. Pow, pow, pow, pow! I ducked and ran to Christian. He flipped me over the back of the couch and said, "Stay down!" He didn't know me and didn't know where I had come from.

Christian and his friends shot back in the crowd. I saw a gun and grabbed it. Right when I called out to Christian, I saw a man walking through the club with a mask on and a gun. As people began scrambling, I shot at him twice. "Farren what the fuck," I heard Greg yell. They shot in my direction and the man came down. Christian looked at me with red in his eyes. "Go home," he yelled. "Aye, get her home," he told some little dude. "I can get myself home," I jerked my arm back. How dare he scold me when I saved his fuckin' life and damn near lost my future. I'm a future attorney; I can't be shooting in no club. I should have stayed my ass home.

"Farren?" He looked at me as if he was saying "don't try me tonight".

I was pissed off to the max; however, I obeyed him and went home. Christian was a liar. There was no way in hell someone who claimed to only do construction and buy investment properties would be getting shot at in the club. I wasn't new to the streets, I grew up in them. Those were trained professionals.

They knew exactly who their target was. I heard people calling Christian, "Boss", when I was headed back to my car.

"I'm good, I don't need you to follow me in." My pleas fell on deaf ears. Two dudes, who I assumed worked for Christian, patrolled my apartment before allowing me to go in. They then told me they would be outside until they heard otherwise from Christian.

Christian

We paid security and a few folks still standing around the club, to say they didn't witness anything happened. With all this shit that happened, I had a migraine. "I'll hit y'all tomorrow," I told my dudes and dapped them up.

"Tomorrow? We need to handle this tonight," Tyrone, one of the lieutenants said. We had pulled over on a dead street.

"The streets are too hot. Let's get up tomorrow," Greg said. I hopped in my Range and pulled off. I kept calling Farren phone only for her to have me blocked. I drove past her house; there was no way I was sleeping without her. I banged on the door. "I'll sit here all night," I told my security guards who were laughing at me. Her neighbors started opening their doors, but I didn't give a fuck. "This girl is crazy", I told them shaking my head.

"Yes sir she is", one of them replied.

She finally opened the door looking good as hell, but irritation was all over her face. "Wassup?"

"Can I come in?" I asked.

"No sir." She attempted to close the door.

"I'm tired," I told her. "Well go home." She attempted to close the door, again.

I was tired of playing games. I pushed the door back with a little force and waltzed in. "Why you mad?" I asked, following her into her bedroom. "First of all, I tried to help you and you treated me like a child. Secondly, why do you have a fucking gun? And third, what is it that you do, and don't lie to me," she spoke calmly; too calm for my liking.

"Farren, you could have gotten yourself killed. What were you thinking?" I asked her and ignored her line of questioning.

"I was trying to protect you," she yelled.

"I don't need you to protect me, I got me," I yelled back. I hated yelling, especially at the woman I cared for.

She looked at me. "Wow," she said.

"That's not how I meant it. You are a woman; it is my job to protect you, Farren. Don't ever do that again," I came at her.

She walked back. "You can either sleep on the couch or leave." She got into bed and cut the light off.

I didn't come here for this shit. I just knew I was going to fuck her tonight; all this stress had me needing to let one off. I acted like she was in charge and while I was on the couch, I thought who was this stupid nigga that tried to come at us and why? I gave Farren a few more minutes to get her mind right, took all my clothes off and went to her bedroom.

She laid in bed with her hair all over her head, on her phone; probably on Myspace. She looked up. "I know you don't think you about to get you some tonight," she smacked her lips.

"I apologize," I said stroking my dick, walking towards to her.

"Get out my room," she said. I flipped the covers back. "Bend over," I told her. She looked up at me. "I'm so serious Christian, I am mad at you and I don't believe in make-up sex," she said.

"You're so young; make-up sex is the best sex, bae." I pulled her out the bed and placed her on all fours. I went to put my dick in, and she eased back. I took a deep breath. "Farren, I'm not playing no more," I told her. "Eat my pussy and shut up," she told me.

That was all I needed to hear. I kneeled and brought her ass to my face and dived in. "Hmmm, yes," she whispered.

"Ooh, okay, yea, yea," she got louder. I smacked and gripped her ass. I was sure I left handprints on that red fat ass. After her releasing her sweetness on the tip of my tongue more than twice, I entered her with no remorse. "Ahhhh," I exhaled.

"You like it?" she asked, as she threw it back.

"I love this shit," I told her. She bounced back faster and I knew I wouldn't be able to hold it any longer. I bit my tongue to compose me screaming out like a little girl. I came long and hard inside of her. I was drunk, she was drunk, and that was our first case of make-up sex!

We laid in our lovemaking and I traced her spine with my fingertips. "Why did you shoot?" I asked.

"I saw them coming your way. I was taught to shoot first," she looked up and told me.

"Farren, I don't like that hood shit. I respect where you're from because it made you the woman you are, but I like the scholarly you, the classy you. Shooting in the club - I don't condone that. You got lucky tonight with that shot, and I'm thankful that you looked out for me, but let that be the last time," I told her.

"Whatever you say," she said and rolled over with her back now facing me. I pulled her to me and snuggled my face into the crook of her neck, placing soft kisses on her body. "Let's talk. What's on your mind?"

"What do you do? What do you really do? Don't lie to me anymore," she asked for the millionth time.

I turned her over and looked dead in her eyes and wondered if she could handle it. Staring back into my eyes, she read my thoughts.

"I'm not new to this; I'm not naïve," she said.

"You're also in school to be a lawyer. I will never forgive myself if something happened to you," I said, kissing her on the forehead.

"Answer my question," she said.

"I'm 'The Connect'," I told her, straight like that.

She sat up in the bed, titties out and all. "What does that mean?" she asked.

I laughed. "I thought you weren't naïve".

"No, like for real...are you like the Pablo Escobar of Philly?" she questioned.

"No, I'm the Christian Knight of Philadelphia and a few other cities and states"

"So are you really an architect?"

"You think I just walk around with blueprints in my truck for Halloween? Of course it's real. I went to college; I'm not dumb,"

"I never said you were, but for you to be risking your life being 'The Connect' and you're already successful, something isn't right," she shook her head.

"We good, baby, cause I'm tired of talking about this." I ignored her. Either she was about to be with me, or she wasn't; it was simple as that.

A few minutes later, after twirling her hair, putting pajamas on, biting her lip, and twiddling her fingers, she said "Yes daddy." She kissed me in the mouth and I held her 'til we fell asleep.

I woke up to an empty bed. "I'm out boo, got a lot to do today. I'll catch up to you. Key is in kitchen drawer; be safe," a note said that was left on the bathroom mirror and I found when I went in there to take care of my hygiene.

I pulled up to the barbershop. It was Wednesday, but wasn't nothing happy about this hump day.

"So how are we getting to the bottom of this?"

"I don't even know who it could be."

"I bet it's those Jamaicans"

I didn't say much. All I thought was I'm ready for this to be over; I'm done with this lifestyle. I had legit businesses, I owned a successful architecture company, and I enjoyed what I did.

"Let's figure out who it was and y'all call me when y'all get some names...legit names." I didn't have time to sit around and boggle minds all day; I had other shit to handle.

After back-to-back meetings and overseeing groundbreaking, I ended up at my sister, Courtney's house for dinner. Courtney and I were very close.

I walked in and immediately began tossing my nephews in the air. "Where's Derrick?" I asked. "Who knows and who cares." My sister used to hide her hate towards Derrick; now it was all out in the open. I kept telling her to stick it out for the kids, but she wasn't trying to hear that.

"Y'all good sis?" I asked.

"Nope, but how are you and Miss Farren?" She brought me a beer and joined me on the couch.

"We're good. That's my baby." I smiled and shot her a text.

"Is she the one?" Courtney asked.

"Oh yeah, most def," I said with no hesitation. She looked at me. "For real, Chrissy?"

I laughed. "Yes Courtney, she's the mother of my kids."

"What about law school and all that? She's not working that hard to sit at home and have your babies."

"We haven't even talked about all of that yet, but it will work out," I told her.

"I'm happy for you, you deserve it," she said as she hugged my neck.

"I'm about to get on out of here," I said when I heard Derrick's truck pull up in the driveway.

"Don't leave," she whined.

"I'll come scoop you this weekend and we can hit the casino," I told her.

"I need a break; that sounds like a plan. Don't cancel," she told me.

I left her house and headed home. Today was a long day with a longer night. There was nothing more I wanted now than a shower, a drink and a blunt. I called Farren when I got in the car. "Hello," she whispered.

"I've been texting you," I told her.

"You know I started back classes today, plus worked and I went in 255 for a minute," she mumbled.

"What you go in there for?" As soon as we started talking, I asked her not to work there anymore. People drinking alcohol and getting mad – I'd have to come up there and kill one of them niggas.

"They were training a bartender and needed a lil' help. Nothing major bae," she yawned.

"How was class?'

"It's going to be hard, but I'm confident I'mma be working hard baby; all A's," she told me.

"If it's too much, you let me know; if you wanna feel like you're working, I'll find you a lil' office job with set hours," I told her.

"Thanks baby, I got it for now."

"How did you sleep last night?" I asked her.

"I always sleep well when I'm sleeping next to you," she said, causing me to smile.

"I'm missing you baby," I told her. With her I was weak and mushy, and I didn't care; she brought me so much joy.

"I miss you more. Let's try and meet up this weekend." Today was Wednesday; I didn't know if I could wait that many days. "Okay, I'm taking Courtney to the casino this weekend," I told her.

"Oh, well have fun boo," she said.

"No, you're coming; it's all of us," I told her.

"Oh okay, baby," she replied.

"I know you gotta wake up in the a.m.; hit me on your break," I told her. "Goodnight

Christian." "Night ma, one." I disconnected the call, and focused on getting home safe.

Chapter 4

Christian's Birthday Night

Farren

"Ma, you okay?" Christian knocked on the door.

"Yes, gon' and go out. Ashley is here, I'll be fine." I was prowled over the toilet.

"Let me in," he demanded.

"No Christian, bye," I told him and I threw up again. It was the beginning of October and it was Christian's 36th birthday. We planned a week of small gatherings and outings and next week we were taking a quick trip to Vegas.

Ashley came in a few minutes later. "Bitch, you know you pregnant?"

I shot her the middle finger. "Shut up."

"Farren, I told you when you got me from the airport, you look fat as hell. What are you going to do?" she asked, wiping my face and helping me up.

"I don't want children right now. I'm focused."

"Honey if you were focused, you wouldn't be having sex without a condom," she got on me.

I took some medicine and lay down; I would confirm everything after the birthday plans were over. Saturday night was to be epic.

Ashley and I spent the day getting pampered. I was paying for our massages when Christian texted and my sister called three times. I checked my inbox.

"Baby, I miss you."

The text from Neeki read, "How many people can I bring with me?"

A text from Courtney said, "Hey sis! I got the cake; let me know if I can do anything else.

My mother sent a text stating she wanted to go visit her sister in a few weeks, and the tickets were $340.00.

Some chic named Muff said she got my number from Neeki and wanted to know could she use my discount to purchase some shoes when she got paid.

The last one from Greg read, "What up sis? This man is getting weary; he trying to come home and check on you!"

I sat there and replied to all of my messages.

To Christian: "I miss you more, Daddy."

To Neeki: "1."

To Courtney: "I'm headed to pick up his gift now; thanks sis, see you tonight."

To Mom: "Okay ma, I will drop money off Monday; love you 2."

To Muff: "It's an extra $100 to use my discount; call before you come to make sure I'm there. Please don't give my number out."

To Greg: "Take him to the cigar shop or something. Lock him down for three more hours."

"Girl, come on." I slid in the Range, and we headed to pick up my baby's gift. I'd been saving all my money to get him the perfect gift, and I really hoped he enjoyed the sincerity of it.

Neeki called me. "Girl, what the fuck does my sister want?"

"Wassup Neeki?" I said.

"Why can I only bring one person with me?" she asked with attitude.

"Because it's not my birthday, its Christian's, and this is for his family and friends," I explained.

"Girl okay, whatever," she said and hung up.

"I can't wait to see lil' Neeki," Ashley joked. I rolled my eyes at her.

The phone rang again, and this time it was from Christian's worrisome self. "Hey bae," I said as I got into traffic.

"I haven't seen you in four days," he whined.

"I know, I've been working doubles at work," I lied. I'm really getting fat as hell, and I didn't want him to notice.

"You coming to the club tonight?" he asked for the millionth time today.

"Yes Christian," I said as my line clicked. "Bae, I'mma call you back," I said. "I love you," he said.

"Huh? Chris, I'mma call you back."

I whispered, "Christian said he loved me." My eyes popped out.

"You're already pregnant, so what's the problem?" Ashley laughed.

"Hello Ms. Walters, we are here now decorating. To confirm, the boat will dock at 10 p.m. correct?" the party coordinator asked.

"Yes ma'am."

I planned Christian an all-white boat party that would dock in New York, and his party would be at the 40/40 club. The boat ride was intimate and for his close personal friends, business associates and family members. It featured a jazz band, deejay and catered food.

It was 8:30 when I got in the shower. My hair was pressed, and I made sure it was wrapped super tight. Ashley bathed in the other room since we were rushing. My phone had been ringing off the hook all day. I wasn't able to return everyone's text because I had too much to do. While the makeup artist did my makeup, I scanned and replied to messages.

Greg: "We're leaving the shop from playing dice; going to change now."

Courtney: "Headed there now."

Chloe: "I'm here... place looks great, you did your thing girl."

Neeki: "It's just me, Candace, Tasha and KoKo."

Sid: "Can't wait to see you tonight; it's been forever."

255 bar: "I found someone else to help me bartend for $500."

I replied:

Greg: "Okay, I'm getting dressed; text when you pulling up. Just say it's one of your boo's birthdays."

Courtney: "Okay sis, I'm running late; makeup artist was late!

Chloe: "Thanks! We're turning up tonight!"

I didn't even bother replying to Neeki; she just didn't listen to me.

Sid- "Yes, we about to turn up and Ashley is here!"

255 bar- "For two hours? No, $250."

My makeup was flawless. I slid on a cranberry dress by Dolce; it was halter and stopped mid-thigh. My teal Alexandar McQueen python heels were going to be a killer in the morning, but I wore them for my baby anyway! And the finishing touch was my bone-straight hair.

"Oh look at you, baby mama," Ashley squealed. She had been waiting in the rental car for a few minutes. "Please don't call me that," I said sadly.

"Farren your stomach is poking," she pointed. I looked down and I noticed the tiny baby bump that was forming. "Oh my goodness, I gotta grab a jacket."

"Girl we are already too late, and it's not that cold yet," she told me.

My phone was going ham; I didn't even respond to anyone. I was too busy being pissed that the driver didn't know his way around Philly.

When I got there, Christian had already walked and I missed the "SURPISE" part. I was so frustrated and mad that I missed his facial expressions once he saw his family and friends were here to celebrate his birthday.

"I'm so sorry; it was so much traffic, my makeup artist was late, traffic..." I attempted to explain. He grabbed me up in a bear hug and he kissed me all over.

"You're the best, bae," he told me. It was evident he was already toasted.

"I gotta go check on everything." He pulled me back to him. "Say Christian, I love you," he commanded. With no hesitation I said, "Christian, I love you more than anything." He smiled, kissed me again and watched me as I walked off.

"Farren!" Neeki yelled at me. "I just got here, let me tell the conductor we can go," I told her.

"You look pretty, bitch," she told me.

"Thanks girl, so do you," I replied. Once I made sure everything was good, I found my way to Ashley and my line sister, Sid. "Farren girl you getting thick," she commented.

"Good eating," I half lied.

In a corner, Neeki and her childhood friends stood and looked at Christian and all his friends turning up and rolling up. "Your sister's boyfriend is fine as hell."

"Girl, ain't he? I already know," Neeki replied.

"Farren look pregnant too... I wasn't going to say anything but uhh," Neeki's friend Ko said.

She looked over at her and instantly saw the bump forming. Little Miss Perfect done got knocked up.

Christian

"Is Farren pregnant?" Courtney whispered in my ear. "Huh?" I was drunk but I wasn't that damn drunk.

"Christian look at her," she exclaimed. I haven't really seen her this week or last week since she's been busy with school and working. I looked at her, and walked in her direction but was cut short. "Christian, do a toast; we about to dock in New York and there are limos waiting to escort people to the club then strip club." I looked surprised. The coordinator said, "I thought you knew; don't tell Farren I told you." She handed me the microphone and signaled the band to cut it short.

"Yo, mic check one, two, one, two.... I just want to thank all y'all for coming out to celebrate with me tonight; my niggas, my beautiful sisters, my partners, my business associates, colleagues, cousins, clients, lil' kids from the block, but most importantly, first and foremost - my baby, my best friend. I think she about to be baby mama, I ain't figured that out yet." Farren turned beet red. "I love you mama, and everything about you; turn the fuck up, everything on me tonight."

Everybody cheered and we took shots. Farren was busy making sure the party was running smoothly. We took the rentals to the 40/40 club where bottles were ready to be popped, and the cake to be cut. We turned up all night! I texted Farren once I was ready to leave.

"Where you bae?"

"At the hotel."

"We got a room?"

"Everybody does, boo."

"Where 'bout? I'm ready to come kiss you."

"Enjoy your night; we have forever to do that."

"I wanna be with you. Room number?"

"Three-forty-two; get the key from check-in."

"Love you, baby."

"Love you, too. Happy Birthday."

I dapped my niggas, told them I was out, and kissed my sisters. "Farren got everybody rooms, y'all too drunk to be driving!"

"Nigga we know, she planned this months ago."

"Be safe sis," I told Courtney. Greg said, "I got her bruh," as he smiled. I smiled back and dapped him up. "My nigga."

Baby girl was already knocked out when I got in. I barely made it to the shower from being drunk. This was the best birthday I'd ever had.

"Bae," I shook her.

"Christian, I love you. I'm so tired baby," she whined.

"Okay baby, I just wanna hold you," I slurred.

Drunk sleep was the best sleep, especially when you was able to go to bed and wake up to the woman of your dreams.

Farren

Ashley and I were up early the next morning; brunch was at 2 p.m., downstairs in one of the ballrooms. I wore an olive green wrap dress and Gucci sandals. His name was on each of the menus. Christian entered, and on this beautiful Sunday morning in his khaki suit and shades, he looked amazing. I watched him kiss and greet his parents. I'm sure he was surprised to see all his aunties and stuff, but this was truly a family affair.

"You have really outdone yourself," he kissed me on the cheek. The brunch was great; a poet came, violinist played and everyone was able to feast on a Southern buffet.

"When are we going to talk?" he asked me on the drive back to Jersey. Ashley looked at me and pretended to not be present.

"Doctor's appointment in the morning at 10 a.m.," I told him.

I was happy my baby enjoyed his weekend. I went to the study and locked myself in there until the wee hours of the morning. I was determined to finish this semester with a 4.0 and nothing less.

Christian was up before me the next morning. "Baby wake up, I made you some tea." He was all in my face.

I rolled over. "What time is it?" I know I didn't climb into bed until two or three, up with Ashley all night. I wanted to talk about life and she wanted to think of baby names.

"It's 8:00."

"Christian, the doctor is twenty minutes away. Why are you up so early?" I asked from under the pillow.

"We gon' be on time," he said, snatching the covers from me. "I ran you a bath." He pulled me out of bed and stripped me naked.

As I bathed, he rolled up and sat on the toilet. "No privacy this morning?" I asked.

"Nope. Bae, thank you for everything, man," he looked at me and smiled.

"You had fun for real?"

"Yeah boo, I wasn't expecting any of that."

I washed in between my legs. "Did you ever open up your gift?" I asked him. He looked up. "You got me a gift, too?"

I couldn't help but laugh. "Go look in my overnight bag."

He came back and sat on the toilet. By now I was drying off and brushing my teeth. I didn't hear anything for a few seconds; my heart kind of stopped. "You don't like it?"

He looked up at me with misty eyes. "This means everything to me," he said above a whisper.

He scanned through the photo book of our photos and love sayings together over the last ten months; photos in black and white, some in color, hotel receipts and movie ticket stubs.

He stood behind me and ran his hand through my hair; he preferred it wild and all over my head like a lost child.

"I love you so much," he told me. He took the towel away and entered me from behind; I couldn't do anything but hold on for the ride.

"Hmm, babyyyyy," he moaned in my ear. I spread my legs a little wider and received the blessing he was offering.

"Yes, yes, come on, Daddy," I spoke back. He gripped my waste gently but with force, and slanged that dick all in me until he released.

"Ahhh," he yelled once he pulled out. He took his time washing me back up before he entered the shower. I slid on Uggs and a Nike jogging suit, since the weather was slightly bipolar in Philly.

Christian wore jeans, a V-neck and a blazer; he was so hood-corporate. Ashley put her bags in the trunk; my sis was leaving today. It seems as if the week went by too fast.

In the car, Christian's phone rang nonstop. "We're headed there now bruh." Greg called, and then Courtney, Chloe, and his aunts; it must have dawned on everyone now that hangovers were over.

"Farren Walters," the nurse called me back.

"Ashley, come on," I told her. "Are you sure?" Christian ushered her in as well.

We patiently waited on the doctor to come back. After tests were ran, the doctor came in. "Okay Farren, yes you are pregnant. Let's see how many weeks you are," Dr. Taliaso said. Christian smiled and kissed my forehead. She spread the cold gel across my midsection, and a few seconds later we heard something that sounded like a thump in an ocean of water – the baby's heartbeat. "Oh my God." Tears rolled down my face; I couldn't believe an angel was growing inside of me.

I looked at Ashley and she was crying, too. "I'm so happy for you. I have to go outside," she said wiping away tears.

"Ms. Walters, you are approximately fourteen weeks which gives you a due date of March 8th. We can probably get a glimpse of the baby's sex before Thanksgiving. Here are your pre-natals, and congratulations again." She shook Christian's hand, and handed us an envelope with the 3d ultrasound.

"How do you feel?" I asked him. "You're about to make me a father; I'm more than happy right now, baby." He kissed me passionately and wiped my tears.

"You don't think we're moving too fast?" I don't know why all of a sudden I was being insecure.

He looked at me. "Girl, no; I've been asking you to move in with me, so you know you don't have a choice now," he smiled.

"I just don't want things to change. I don't want you to start cheating on me because I'm getting fat," I cried.

"Farren, shut up. So does that mean we're together now?"

"Yes," I said with a smile. He helped me get dressed and we met Ashley in the lobby.

"Ashley, it was nice meeting you," Christian told my best friend, as I dropped him off at his office. He had turned up last week. He said without his car this week, he would be forced to get shit done.

"See you later, baby mama," he kissed me. "Boy bye!" I replied.

We rode to our old hood before it was time for her flight. "Girl, I'm so glad we got out of here," she said as we parked.

"Me and you both."

"You remember when Wanda got locked up?" she asked.

"Girl, you know I do. I need to send her some money." Wanda was the diva in our hood. All the big time drug dealers used to drop hella dough on her to stash drugs in her house. Wanda was tall and pretty with no kids. She used to let us come to her house and play in her makeup and clothes, and she always had fresh-baked goods. Man, I used to love Wanda. I actually met Dice at her house. When Wanda got locked up, it was like my second mama, big sister, and confidante was all gone.

I used my key to get in my mother's house; she was in the kitchen smoking on a cigarette. "Girl, let me call you back; Farren and her friend just walked in."

My mother was forty-five and tiny. Her skin was as dark as midnight, but it was smooth. She had a head full of thick hair that she always wore in a tight ponytail. My mother worked at the hotel since I was a little girl, and she's been there for twenty-five years. She had never been one to keep a man long, but that was her business. I never got into any of that, because I had my own life and problems.

I've begged my mother to move out this raggedy ass apartment, the same one she raised my sister and I in, but she refused. She liked sitting outside with the other women being nosey and gossiping. She still sent the corner kids to the store to get the groceries.

"Look at you girl. When's the last time you been to see me?" my mother asked as she hugged Ashley.

"It's been years; you know I hate coming up here, Ms. Nancy."

"Girl you were raised in Hardy, I don't wanna hear that." I shot Ashley a look that said "please don't get her started".

"How are you missy?" my mother asked me.

"I'm good ma, just left the doctor."

"Yeah, I've been waiting on you to come on over here. Neeki told me you were pregnant."

"How did she know; I just found out thirty minutes ago,"

"Mmm hmmm. Are you keeping it?'

Ashley's eyes popped up, and mines damn near popped out my head. "Uh yes, why wouldn't I?"

"You're not even finished with school."

"Okay, and I'm still going to finish school, ma." I don't understand why she was so concerned. I had never asked for a dime for my education.

"Have one baby you'll have another one and another one. That man done lived his life. He's ready for a wife and children."

"And ma, that's fine; I'm ready for all that, too," I popped back. I loved Christian and as long as I was happy, that's all that should matter to her.

"Don't be a fool, Farren."

"I'm not, I'm good. I'm twenty-six with a job and in school. I moved out when I was seventeen, and have been handling myself ever since. I've never asked you for anything."

"Nooooo, missy, because niggas been handling shit for you, don't forget it."

"Farren, let's go."

"Yeah before I forget you're my mother and do you," I said while looking her dead in the eyes.

"Leave my money," she said, or rather demanded.

I shook my head and peeled five, crisp hundreds off for her and laid them on the kitchen table. I was giving her a thousand but fuck that. With tears welled up in my eyes I said, "You enjoy your trip." I knew it would be a long time before I stepped back in that apartment.

My sister wondered why I clung to Christian's sisters and my line sisters, and took trips with them and hung with them; it was because they were genuine and sweet, not loud and alley. They cared about me. My mother and sister were always trying to prove some invisible ass point.

"Farren, your family has been trifling," Ashley shook her head. I attempted to stick the key into the ignition, but my hands trembled tremendously. I was so hurt it was crazy. I burst into tears, and held my stomach. I promised myself then and there I would never treat my son or daughter like that; I would love him or her unconditionally.

"It's okay, boo," she rubbed my back. I wiped my face and rushed to get my friend to the airport.

"I love you more than life. Keep my godchild safe." She hugged me tight, but I was spaced out.

"Call me when you land," I told her.

I went to my condo to start packing up a few things, but I couldn't even function. I kept replaying my mother's hateful words in my head over and over again. It brought back the day Dice told me something so real.

I'll never forget any of the wisdom he instilled in me.

Back in the day

It was after my graduation and the gifts Dice and my daddy had got me, my mother and sister had already claimed half of the stuff.

My mother knocked on the door. "Good morning mommy," I said. I was in the best mood ever. I had just graduated from high school, valedictorian at that.

She pulled on her cigarette. "How much money your daddy left you?"

I sat up in the bed. "What?"

"You heard me; it's bills due around here."

"Okay, if I didn't get graduation money, how else would they have gotten paid?" I asked. I knew then and there I wasn't gon' be in this hell hole much longer.

"Pay the light and cable bill," she said and closed the door.

I called Dice. "Baby, wassup?" he answered on the first ring. "You at home?" I asked.

"Yep. My daughter's pre-k graduation is today," he said in a hushed tone.

"Hit me later," I told him. Hours passed before he texted me and said,
"Pack a bag, I'll be there in 30 mins baby."

When I hopped in his ride he said, "Hey graduate."

"Dice, I gotta move," I blurted.

"What's wrong bae?"

"She took my graduation money, Neeki had on my Michael Kors shoes this morning…. I worked hard for my gifts; it's not fair," I told him.

"Don't worry about that shit. Farren, I been told you, bae, it be the closest ones to you that'll hurt you, and you don't deserve that shit man. Your heart is so big people take your kindness for weakness." He spoke real to me that night, and we had sex through the rest of the night and the next morning.

"Bae I gotta get to the house, but find something you like and text me the address." He kissed me goodbye. I was so tired I didn't even complain that he was leaving.

A few days later, Ashley and I moved into a condo. Her mother's new boyfriend was all the reason she needed to get the hell on. She worked two jobs the summer before we started school.

I looked around my condo and I couldn't believe I had been living here nine years. It was time for new beginnings; but something in me told me to never let it go.

Chapter 5

Christian

"It has been an honor working with you on this project," Celeste, the owner of the restaurant I've been diligently designing and constructing, said to me with tears in her eyes. We stood in the middle of the restaurant. In a few minutes, guests would be seated and one of her lifelong dreams will have come true.

"Mr. Knight, I promise the money we make tonight is all yours," she assured me.

"I told you don't worry about that; me being partner is enough." I offered her a smile and walked off.

Celeste was a great girl. Her husband had dreams of opening a five-star Southern cuisine restaurant, something that Philly desperately needed. Midway through the construction he fell ill, and money for constructing the restaurant went to trying to preserve his life. He was a good

man; always was on time and never missed a
meeting. I had a heart; I couldn't leave this lady
out cold with nothing to her name. In her
husband's legacy, together we opened
"Harold's."

I sat at the bar sipping a glass of wine. "Is
this seat taken?" some woman whispered in my
ear. Her hair brushed against my shoulder.

"I'm waiting on my girlfriend, but you can
warm it up for her," I offered her a smile.

"Hmmm... but what can I do for you?" she
asked.

"It depends on how much money you came
with. I would like a drink," I flirted back.

"Let me guess... Hennessy and Coke."

I smirked, "How did you know?"

Farren burst out laughing. "Oh, I know
what you like nigga." Farren took off her coat

and kissed my cheek, as I stood up and pulled her into a hug. "How was your day, lady?"

"Long and tiring, but I couldn't miss your big day for anything," she said.

"Who are they?"

"A few of my classmates. We passed a pop quiz yesterday. Of course I can't drink, so I told them drinks on me," she pouted. I kissed her forehead and rubbed her stomach. "How is my princess doing?" We found out a week before Thanksgiving we were having a daughter, and I couldn't be any happier.

"She's been fussing all day," she said.

"Did you order the food or you decided to bring something?" I asked her. We didn't celebrate Thanksgiving on Thanksgiving because my dad was in the hospital, so we were having Thanksgiving tomorrow on a cold, Sunday afternoon, at my mother's house.

"Christian, I been at work all day and went straight to school, woke up this morning and worked a nine hour shift, and you asking me about some damn peach cobbler?" she snapped.

I took another sip of my drink. This baby was giving her mood swings all the time. "I'll handle it, boo," I told her and rubbed the top of her hand. My phone rung and I looked down before I answered it. It displayed unknown number; decline. She looked over at me but didn't make a comment. I can only imagine what she was thinking.

"Celeste, this is my girlfriend Farren; Farren, this is Celeste," I introduced the two women.

"I love the place and congratulations," she smiled.

"It's all thanks to Christian. I told him you all should have the baby shower here," Celeste offered.

She looked around. "That sounds like a good idea," she said.

"You like that idea, for real?" I asked her.

"Yes, I do. I think that would be nice," she smiled. This chick was super bipolar.

"Hmmm." She rubbed her stomach, and I rubbed it with her. "My boo boo acting up," I said, making baby noises. "Christian don't talk to her like that. We are going to talk to her like she's a big girl." I didn't comment. That was my daughter and I'd talk to her however I wanted to.

"You look beautiful," I smiled at her. "Thank you, Christian." She attempted to conceal her blush. My girl was fly without trying. She wore her hair bone straight with a part in the middle, and her business attire looked casual and sexy on her. We would have to be getting her maternity clothes soon, but I wouldn't bring that up right now.

"What will you have today?" the waiter asked us once we switched to a booth.

"We will have Parmesan Chicken, Au Gratin Potatoes and Steamed Broccoli," I ordered.

"Christian, I wanted steak," Farren told me once the lady left.

"You don't need that bae," I told her. We enjoyed dinner discussing our day and who we would endorse for mayor in a few months.

After dinner and giving her a tour of the restaurant, we drove through the city holding hands and listening to slow jams.

"I love that place, and their food was good!" She praised Harold's once more.

"Yeah it was good; I just hope they stay consistent"

"They will; she's doing this for her husband"

"What you going to do for yours tonight when we get home?" I looked at her with a smirk on my face.

"Honey, nothing but run his bath water. I'm so sleepy," she yawned.

"Awww...damn baby," I fake pouted.

I increased my speed and got us home in twenty minutes.

Once we were in bed, Farren said, "I love you," as I hugged her from behind. "I love you too, baby," I told her. She snuggled closer and sooner than later, was breathing lightly. I said a silent prayer to God, thanking Him for peace and love, for safety and for my girl and our daughter. To have someone to love you and care for you is nothing I take for granted. Every day we spend together is a day that was worth every heartbreak, setback and disappointment I ever experienced before I met Farren; my best friend, my soul mate, my everything.

I would do anything in life to protect her from hurt harm or danger; she meant the world to me. I had the perfect ring designed and I knew she would love it. I was waiting on Christmas morning to propose. I wanted it to be a day she would never forget.

Farren

We were holding hands as Christian drove to his parents' house for Thanksgiving dinner. We had just left a beautiful church service at the church he grew up in, and I was truly still basking in God's glory. I was the happiest girl in the world right now, minus my baby, kicking constantly. We sung along with the radio, and eyed each other under our matching Tom Ford glasses. Christian swore up and down he wasn't mushy, but he was always coming in the house with something matching. We had matching shades, watches, bracelets, necklaces, luggage, pajamas, and the list goes on.

"You make me happyyyyyyy," he belted out. "This yo song or nah?" I asked him. He was rubbing my hand with one hand and snapping his finger with the other, while driving with his knees. I always told him he was a country boy at heart.

"You don't know nothing about this youngin'," he joked.

"Boy please, I grew up on all this. I stayed at the skating rink," I said rocking to the beat.

He took a phone call on his business line and handled the matter with expertise. He kindly informed the client he didn't handle business on Sundays, before disconnecting the call. I turned in my chair. This man was so sexy; I couldn't wait to get him home. Christian clenched his jaw, which warned me that something was wrong but he didn't bring it up, so I didn't either. I knew how to stay in my place and respect my man. Christian protected me and I loved him for it.

His muscles shone through the tailor made suit. We complimented each other so well that I had to post a picture this morning on Myspace. We wore black with a hint of coral and the caption read "1+1=3". Everybody from classmates, people from the hood, sorors, and co-workers all commented, "Omg... I can't believe it. I'm so happy for you." Needless to say, I was in a great mood today and I was confident nothing could take this happiness.

"I can't wait to eat that peach cobbler," Christian told me.

"It's a pan at the house bae, don't be greedy," I told him. Before he could reply, my phone buzzed. I hesitated before answering. "Hey girl, wassup?" I answered my sister's phone call on the very last ring.

"Hey sister, how are you?" she asked cheerfully.

"No complaints my way, and you?" I asked.

"Just did a double shift, headed to take ma to lunch."

"Oh okay, y'all enjoy," I told her.

"We will. You can come meet us if you want. I want to see that belly," she told me.

"Girl, I don't know; work and school kicking my ass," I told her. Christian eyed me.

"Christian is making you work?"

"No, he's not making me do anything. I work because I love my job, Neeki," I told her. My eyes had damn near rolled to the back of my head, twice.

"Oh okay. Well I wanted to give you your baby shower. We need to do lunch soon to plan it," she said. I looked at the phone and placed it back to my ear. *Tuh,* I thought to myself.

"You need to call Ashley and Christian's sisters; they've already been working on it," I told her, "Mmm hmm. Okay sister, 'blood sister', what are you doing today? You gon' meet us?" she asked.

"No, me and Christian are having dinner with his parents," I informed her.

"Honey, hang that phone up and stop begging her," I heard my mama say in the background.

"Okay, y'all enjoy y'all day," I said and hung up.

"What was that about?" Christian asked.

"Nothing worth mentioning; come on baby," I told him. Kennedy, Courtney's daughter ran up to me. "Auntie, I missed you." I picked her up. "You missed me? I just saw you yesterday when we went to get our toes polished," I whined back to her.

"I still missed you." I put her down and she led me to the kitchen with the rest of the ladies.

I looked back and my baby was right behind me.

"Hi family," I greeted Christian's mother and his sisters.

"Hi Farren." They all greeted differently, but with warm smiles.

Christian spoke and went to join his father in the living room.

"How is the baby?"

"She's going to be a daddy's girl. Every time Chris shows me attention, she starts kicking profusely," I poked my stomach out.

His mother smiled. "Chloe was the same way." I already knew that from how she clung to her father; it was very obvious she adored him.

We all helped out bringing dinner to the table. "I would like to say the prayer," I said. Christian looked at me and asked, "Are you sure baby?" I nodded. He looked so surprised. I didn't grow up in a strict Christian household as he did, but I still knew how to pray. His mother smiled and they all joined hands and bowed their heads. Kennedy held my other hand as I cleared my throat a little.

"Father God, I thank you for this day. I thank you for bringing us together under one roof once again, for fellowship and food. I pray that you bless the hands that prepared this food and the hands that bought it. I thank you for good health on today, and more joy and peace. God I know that we have not been brought together in vain. In Jesus' name I pray, amen," I said. The prayer wasn't long and drawn out, but it was heartfelt. I wasn't one of many words but when I did speak it was meaningful.

"Have you all decided on a name?" Courtney asked. We were all full of my homemade peach cobbler, and were lazily laid out on the couch. Christian's parents had retired to their room a long time ago.

"No. Farren likes Madison, and I like Caitlen and Kassidy Nicole Knight."

"Kk.... I love it," Chloe beamed.

"As long as it's with a 'C', he's happy," I told them.

"My sister wants to help with the baby shower. I will text you her number in the morning," I told Courtney.

She looked at Chloe, but they said nothing. "Okay girl," Chloe finally replied.

"Come on boo, let's go; I'm sleepy," Christian said. "Bye ladies," I said and kissed them goodbye.

I texted my sister.

Neeki: "Courtney is going to call you tomorrow."

Neeki: "Okay, I'm excited sis!"

Weeks had passed since we celebrated Thanksgiving dinner with his family. I had been working and focused on finishing the semester strong with at least a 3.5. Christian felt I could push out a 4.0, but my hopes weren't up. I was ready to be done with the semester and celebrating the holidays with my loved ones. Work was work and I never had time to just relax. Another vacation was desperately needed.

"When are you going to slow down?" Christian asked me over the phone. I was at my condo looking for my camouflage Ugg boots; it was freezing in Philly and I wanted to pull them out. I haven't been here in forever. Christian didn't play about me being home and in bed with him every night; Mr. Controlling, himself.

"I have slowed down, Christian. What the fuck do you want me to do, sit around and suck your dick all day?" I spat.

"I'mma talk to you later," he said before he hung up. I didn't even feel like calling him back.

I didn't care to even argue with him today. He always felt like he knew best. He was always trying to tell me what he thought I needed to do, and I didn't want to hear that shit; not today.

I packed up my Uggs and a few of my thermals, and headed to dinner by my damn self. "Damn, I know that's not lil' Farren ducked off back there," I heard someone say. I was six months pregnant and fat. I always had a taste for weird shit and tonight there was nothing else I wanted but a greasy, fat burger from TappOut, a raggedy hole in the wall in the middle of the hood. Christian hadn't called me and I haven't called his ass, either.

"Damn, ma! Come give me a hug." I got up in front of my table and waddled to him slowly. "Damnnnnnn, you pregnant." It was Dice's brother, Dominic.

"Yes, six months. Come sit with me," I told him.

"How have you been? You still in school"

"Yep. I got a year or two left. I'm taking next semester off though" I told him, as I popped an onion ring in my mouth.

"Dice would be so proud of you, ma."

I smiled. "I already know," I told him. We had some good times back in the day.

"Who got you in here iced out and eating by yourself? You trying to get knocked?" he joked.

"He's at work probably, and nah, this is my hood. You know Hardy love me!" I told him.

"Man, Hardy ain't the same," he shook his head. "Food still tastes the same."

"Where are you at now?"

"I still got my condo, ain't shit changed," I told him. Christian would knock me silly if I told someone where we laid our head.

"That's wassup, ma. I'mma get outta here. Stay safe," he told me and I wished him the same.

Minutes later I was headed to my truck...well, it might as well be my truck. I loved Christian's Range Rover.

I headed home with still, no word from Christian, but I didn't care. I had work in the morning and school after that. I was headed straight to the tub, and then bed; that's exactly what I did.

Little did I know, Christian was somewhere ending innocent people's lives.

Christian

"I promise I don't know where he is," the lady cried. She was beat to a bloody pulp; this shit was crazy.

Greg hit her in the knee with a baseball bat. "Yo, chill out," I hissed.

I didn't want to be here. I wanted to be at home fucking my girl, not yelling at some innocent lady who didn't know where her sorry ass boyfriend was. She was young and dumb; she only knew what he told her. This woman was not the one to blame, but telling my circle that was like talking to a brick wall. I sat in the corner, smoking a blunt, ready to go.

Greg looked at me and laughed. "This nigga! You act like you fuckin' her." The rest of them laughed, too.

I had been here for hours and I was done for the night. "I'll holla at y'all niggas later." I left and headed home.

Farren was sleeping peacefully as I kneeled by her side of the bed, and kissed her stomach. "Daddy gon' get it together just for you, baby," I told my daughter.

"Where have you been?" she whispered with her eyes closed.

"I had to handle something," I kissed her forehead. "I'm sorry about earlier," she mumbled.

"Well quit your job," I told her. She started fake-snoring. "Nah, your ass ain't sleep, get up!" I tickled her. "Stop, my stomach already hurting," she winced.

"What's wrong?" I asked. The doctors had been telling Farren over and over that her workload was too heavy and the baby was always in distress, but Miss Independent just couldn't sit down.

"I ate a burger from Tappout." I took a deep breath. The guy we were looking for was from Hardy. "Farren, I need you to stay from over there, okay baby?" I told her. "I'm from Hardy Projects. I grew up there and so did my mama; I'm good out there," she sassed me.

"Farren, I'm looking out for us and our baby," I touched her cheek.

She didn't say anything. "I don't want to lock you down, but I will." I made sure she felt my tone through my words, and understood that I was dead ass serious.

"Good night. We have a doctor's appointment in the morning, and we are going to start on Christmas shopping; it will be here before we know it." I re-tucked her in the bed and went to take a long shower. I knew I was having a drink before I went to sleep; it had been a long day. I was on the couch sprawled out, catching some reels from tonight's game, while smoking a blunt and drinking some Dusse. My phone rang and it was my sis.

"What up sis?" I asked Courtney. It was four in the morning.

"Hey, what are you doing?" she asked.

"Watching the game," I told her. I was a calm man; I never pressed people to talk about what was on their mind. People felt more comfortable talking when they were ready to.

"Chrissy, I fucked up," she whispered.

"What you mean?" I asked.

"I'm pregnant," she whispered.

"Where are you? Why are you whispering?" I asked.

"I'm sitting in my car. I just got off work," she told me.

"This late?"

"I had to postpone a surgery for a case study, 'til tonight." My sister was my role model. She was always working hard, doing research and performing surgeries that most surgeons would be scared to perform.

"Come to the house," I told her, and she informed me she was already outside.

I opened the door to let her in. She looked tired, weak and distraught. I hugged her as she cried continuously, releasing all of her pain. "Baby, is everything okay?" Farren asked from the top of the balcony. She looked so beautiful in one of my t-shirts, with her big belly sticking out, face fat and feet swollen; my own personal angel.

"Yes baby, go back to sleep; we have an early morning." I gave her the look. She looked at Courtney once more before returning to our master bedroom.

I led her to the kitchen. "Are you hungry? Farren threw down the other day."

"No, I'm good. She's always cooking," she said, attempting to lighten the mood.

"Why are you crying? You're not happy about the pregnancy?" I asked. It was no secret that me and my Courtney have always chased success over everything else, but I was getting old; I wanted as many kids as I could get out of Farren. Courtney balanced her family and work well, but I'm not sure if she could do it without the help of Chloe and my mother.

"It's by Greg," she stated as she looked at me.

"Does he know?"

"No. I've been calling him all night and can't reach him. Have you seen him today?"

I nodded. "We had to handle something; he'll probably call you in the morning. I just got home not too long ago, myself." I confirmed her suspicions. I knew Greg really cared about my sister but he was a "hot boy"; he loved this street shit. I wasn't really sure he wanted a family, or a kid.

"Do you plan on keeping it?" I asked.

She twirled her wedding ring around and sighed. "Chrissy, I love my family and I love my kids. Kennedy's getting older, and the boys - they're starting football soon. But it's my happiness that's in question. What about me? I'm not happy," she sighed.

"Your happiness is important, but how you're going about this, is all wrong. Greg loves the streets; you wanna bring your kids around that life? You are a doctor - an educated female. That's who you wanna be with, a drug dealer?" I asked her.

She looked at me. "Aren't you the pot calling the kettle black?" she asked.

"I'm just saying, I know what I'm doing and I don't bring the streets to my home. I don't even discuss that life with Farren; I'm over this street shit anyway," I told her.

No one could tell me that living in the streets didn't end in anything other than jail or a casket because I would tell them to wake up and get real. I'll be damned if I put my family in harm's way for me being greedy for more money; I had enough. I budgeted and I saved. The streets didn't owe me anything. No one was loyal, no one cared about you, and anybody would turn on you if the price was right. I lived by a solid code: make enough money to last for more than rainy days, money for my family, money for investments if they go wrong, money for my children's children, and money for trips. If I wanted to wake up and go to Paris, I could do that. I struggled enough growing up and I vowed to never be broke again.

"I've heard that before." She gathered her things. "I love you, brother. I'll handle this situation." She kissed my cheek and left.

I called Greg's phone and it went straight to voicemail. This wasn't my issue; I had enough to deal with on my plate.

"What was going on last night?" Farren asked the next morning, while we both got dressed to begin our day.

"Nothing for you to worry about," I told her. I slid on a thermal, jeans and my timberlands.

"Can you zip these up for me?" She flopped on the bed, as I stood before her and took care of her shoes.

"I never thought we would be here... celebrating birthdays, Thanksgiving and now Christmas," she smiled. This pregnancy had her so emotional. Farren was usually a bull dog. "It's so much more in store, baby," I told her. I tucked my gun in the front of my jeans; she looked but didn't say anything. Farren know when to be quiet and when to speak, and I loved that most about her. She handled her business and minded mine.

"Who all are we getting gifts for?" she asked once we pulled up to valet the car at the mall.

"My sisters, nieces and nephews, business associates, my assistant and her daughter, ma and daddy, and then whoever you need to handle," I told her.

The day was long and tiring. I copped my sisters Gucci bags and shoes, and my nieces and nephews received a $1000 for their savings account along with toys, clothes and bikes. I got my daddy a cigar set and cologne; he was very simple and didn't expect much. I got my mom some silk pajamas and diamond earrings, and all of my business associates received custom made time pieces. Farren picked out my assistant a nice perfume set and a Tory Burch bag, and her daughter, a Victoria Secret gift card.

"I got Ashley's gift; she's going to love this," she told me once we put all the bags in the car.

"Ooh," she winced. It wasn't her first time doing it either. "Wassup ma, you good? Is it the baby?" I asked.

"I'm okay," she told me.

"Let's just go home; we did enough today." I instructed her to get in the car.

"I'm hungry," she hissed.

I laughed and peeled into traffic. "I'mma feed you big girl, just hold on."

My phone rang, and I answered, "Yo."

Greg's voice came through the line. "We have a problem."

"Okay, handle it."

"Nah, you going to want to handle this one yourself; I'll be around the way," and he disconnected the call.

"Let me get you home." I touched Farren's hand and rubbed it; she had her head resting on the headrest.

"Just get me some Wendy's. I'mma catch up on my shows; that's all I want to do today," she said sadly.

"You good?" I asked Farren once I made sure she was comfortable. "Yes baby," she kissed me passionately. I kissed her back and she kissed me again. "Farren I gotta go," I told her. She looked so sad.

"If something happens, then what?" she asked.

I never saw that fear in her eyes before, but at this present time it was definitely there. "I'm coming back to you in a few hours," I told her.

"I don't believe you."

I took her chin in my hands. "I wouldn't hurt or leave you intentionally; if something does happen, just know you are my best friend and I love you more than I love myself," I told her. She kissed me again.

"Stay up for me bae," I yelled from the front door. I hopped in my pickup truck and called Greg. "I'm on the way."

"Bet."

I pulled up to the barbershop and went around to the back. "What up," I said when I entered the basement.

I saw a young boy that couldn't have been older than thirteen. He was beaten so bad, I couldn't even make his image out.

"Who is that?" I asked.

Jason spoke first. "Some young nigga that we caught about to run up in the spot." He kicked him again.

Greg passed me the blunt. "We don't have any enemies, so I don't know who keeps sending young niggas after us."

I shook my head. "Me neither."

"Aye young buck," I said pulling him to his feet. His teeth were missing, one eye busted, and the other swollen. I felt bad for the boy.

"Who sent you?" I asked - no yelling, no hitting. I needed him to think he could trust me and that I wouldn't kill him.

"Fuck you," he spat out blood.

"Why fuck me? You don't even know me," I asked.

"I'm not telling you shit; unlike these pussy niggas in your circle, I'm loyal," he mumbled.

Greg yelled, "Who's not loyal in here? You know something we don't know kid?" he asked.

"Don't worry about it," he laughed. I liked this lil' nigga; he had heart. Even in the midst of him about to die, he was still staying down for whoever sent him.

Jason shot him. "You stupid nigga; that bullet coulda hit me or Christian," Greg yelled.

"He was wasting time. I'll call the cleanup crew," he said and walked out the room.

Tyson, who hadn't said anything the whole night, said, "Y'all need to watch that nigga; he looking real suspect to me."

Greg looked at me and shook his head. "Yo I'm out; y'all stay safe." He dapped me up and pulled me in for a hug. "Ride with me," I told him.

We sat in Houston's for lunch and chopped it up. Greg has been my best friend for almost twenty years; he's that friend that was always down to ride. "How's baby mama doing?" he asked.

"Still working and going to school; won't sit her she's good," I told him.

He nodded. "You like that shit about her!"

I contemplated on making my next statement. "Yo, you remember Dice from hardy projects?" I asked.

"Nigga, who don't remember him? Before I knew what being rich really was, I thought he was living the life."

I nodded my head and kept my comment to myself. "Me too," I told him. Dice had always been a flashy nigga. People from afar used to tell horror stories of him killing on the spot for not having his money, or for it being short. I don't see how Farren dated someone so ruthless, especially at a young age.

"That's Farren's ex-boyfriend, first love and all that bullshit," I added.

He looked up at me. "Are you for real? When did she tell you?" he asked.

"I been knew, but I've been thinking about it a lot lately," I admitted.

"Why?"

"Because the nigga died in front of her and she was fucked up behind it, but she act like she good and... I don't know, I think I'm tripping."

"Hold on, wait.... I thought they said somebody robbed him?"

"They did, well a nigga did. She said it was the best friend, his partner, that nigga pretty Tony. Remember him?"

"Yeah, but didn't Dice's brother kill him?"

"Yeah, but what I want to know is why he killed Dice and didn't search the house and kill her?"

"Bruh, you're digging up too much dirt."

"But I want to know 'cause it's been bothering me. I'm falling in love and she's about to have my child. I even brought a ring. I need to know that a year from now she won't be setting my ass up." I hated to say that out my mouth and I hated to use my fiancé as my reason for my trust issues, because her and Farren were two different people....or were they?

Chapter 6

Farren

Christmas came so fast this year I was elated, and the smile on my face couldn't be wiped off no matter what. I spent the entire week, decorating the house and putting up the Christmas tree. I baked cookies for Santa and drunk all the virgin eggnog my stomach would allow. This time last year, I woke up in a bed alone, bills piled up to the ceiling; I was lonely and wouldn't admit it. I spent the entire holiday in bed watching movies and eating noodles and hot chips.

Present day, I woke up in a million dollar home next to the man of my dreams, with my angel kicking in my stomach. In three months, my daughter would be entering this world. It's amazing how time flies and seasons change. I never thought this would be my destiny. I was mentally prepared to go through life alone.

After brushing my teeth and slipping on a PINK nightie, I prepared breakfast fit for a king: blueberry pancakes, scrambled eggs with cheese, turkey bacon and sausage, grits, and mimosas. Christian came peering down the stairs in nothing but boxers and a smile. "Merry Christmas baby," he kissed me, and held me in his arms.

"I love you; Merry Christmas!" I told him. We kissed once more and ate breakfast. He was quiet. I knew that Christian had a lot going on, but it was the holidays. For once I just wanted his mind to be at peace and at home with me.

"Open your gift." I handed him a small box. "I told you don't get me anything," he said.

Christian was the giver. He was always giving, giving, giving, and never receiving much. I wanted this year to be different. I was so thankful to have him in my life and grateful for the time we spent together; he meant literally, everything to me.

"Farren, this is nice baby." It was a custom Hublot wallet with his initials on the side. "Open this next."

He opened another small box which contained Burberry cuff links encrusted with diamonds.

"Okay, and these, too," I handed him more. He shook his head in awe.

He looked happy to receive the unlimited supply of socks and undershirts. I wasn't so caught up in material stuff. I got him what I knew he needed and complained the most about it, and the other box contained Cuban cigars and Bond cologne.

After he opened his gifts, he gathered the wrapping to throw away. "What time you wanna head over to my mother's house?" he asked.

Not that I was expecting anything...but then again I was. I didn't want it to look obvious, so I bit my tongue and swallowed the pain in my voice. "I'm about to clean the kitchen then I will get dressed," I told him.

"Alright boo," he said.

What was going on? I was very thrown off and confused, but he wanted me to always be laid back and cool, so that's exactly what he was going to get. I was dressed down to the nines in olive green corduroy jeans, an oversized brown sweater and hot pink Uggs. My hair was pulled up in a bun and I think I applied my makeup perfectly today. I wasn't in a good mood at all. I woke up so thankful and so happy, but all I wanted right now was to understand what was going on.

"Merry Christmas," Kennedy told me for the millionth time. Today was a beautiful day, despite Christian spending the entire day in the basement of his parents' house.

"Is everything okay?" Courtney asked.

"I'm not sure," I told her. I wasn't hiding anything; I really didn't know what the issue was. "Christian, I am ready to go," I told him and he said okay. We had been there all day and my feet were killing me.

On the ride back to the home that we shared, it was silent. I honestly couldn't remember where we went wrong or what even happened. It was Christmas for Jesus' sake, and this is definitely not how I wanted to spend it.

"Farren, can we talk?" he asked me. I was quietly meditating in a bubble bath ran by me for me, when usually Christian would run them for me.

"When I get out of the tub we can," I told him, without looking up.

After I took my time enjoying the warmth of the water, the fragrance of the bath oils and aroma of the lavender and vanilla candles, I dried off and slipped on yoga pants and a tee. I found him in the kitchen having a glass of Henn.

"Wassup Christian?" I asked. My spirit told me this conversation wouldn't have a happy ending, so the first wrong thing he said, I was out of there.

"Did you set up Dice to be killed?"

Wow! I couldn't believe this is what he so desperately wanted to discuss. This is why I didn't receive a Christmas gift, why we didn't make love this morning, and why he's acted like a complete ass for the last couple of weeks. I didn't have time for this; I had a career to start and myself to look after.

"What answer are you looking for?" I asked.

He shook his head. "Don't use that lawyer bullshit on me; I want real fuckin answers!" he yelled.

I looked back. "Oh you're mad?" I laughed. I didn't have time to argue a "case" that I knew was nothing, and if he had to wait damn near a year to ask questions that he should have asked in the beginning, this relationship wasn't really worth my time.

"Farren, I can't continue knowing I feel some type of way; I need you to make this right," he said. He looked sincere and like he really was concerned; but if Christian really cared about me and he trusted me, we wouldn't be sitting here having this conversation on Christmas of all days.

"Well let me get my stuff and leave." I stood up and prepared to clean the kitchen one last time before I left a house that I didn't plan on returning to. I didn't believe in love or in happy endings, and I still gave him my all, still moved in, and still had a baby without a ring. I did everything I said I would never do.

"You're not going anywhere, Farren; are you serious right now?" he asked.

"As a motherfuckin' heart attack. I don't play games, and I don't beat around the bush. If you have me in your house, sleeping in your bed and you thinking one day I'm going to set you up, then I should just leave and go back to my own house so you can rest in peace," I told him - no loudness, no anger, and with no hesitation. He didn't say anything. I grabbed my keys and my purse, and left everything in the house. I had plenty of money saved and my condo was still in livable arrangements. As comfortable as I got with him, I never got too comfortable because all good things come to an end.

"I left your key in the bathroom. I'll call you when the baby's due." I grabbed my laptop charger, and a few of my notebooks.

"Farren, this is not how I expected this to go," he stated.

"What did you expect considering the way you approached me, Christian? I told you what happened and for you to second guess me, means you wanted me to admit to a lie, and I'm not clearing your conscious," I told him.

He looked like he lost his best friend. He really didn't know how I rolled; I didn't go back, I didn't rewind, and I don't regret any decision I make because I'm old enough to make the right decision the first time.

"I love you and you're the mother of my child; I don't want you staying by yourself, so I'll sleep in the guest room," he grabbed my purse.

"Oh, I won't be sleeping in this house another night." I shook my head, grabbed my purse back, and headed to the garage in my "ran down BMW" that I haven't driven in weeks.

"You're really about to leave me?" he asked, shockingly.

"Goodbye Christian. Merry Christmas." I peeled out of the driveway and kissed that life goodbye.

Two months later

"Trish, I think I'm going home early today; I'm not feeling to well. I feel my baby all in my back," I winced.

"Are you okay to drive?" my co-manager asked me.

"Yes, yes, I'll be okay. She will be coming any day now," I attempted to smile.

I was as big as a damn house, but this February weather was treating me well. I loved the winter time, but going home to an empty condo every night with swollen feet, was not what I liked. I picked up an extra job as the manager at Express, since I took a semester off to prepare for the arrival of my daughter.

I completely cut off all ties with my family and Christian's. His sisters were very disappointed when I asked them to cancel the baby shower. They insisted that Christian's bullshit didn't interfere with them being proud aunts, but I didn't wanna hear that shit. I lived alone and survived alone for years before I met Christian; I was perfectly fine.

He attempted to contact me a few times, each time being met with the ignore button or no reply to his ever long text message. He continued to send gifts for the baby and me to the apartment. I accepted the baby gifts, but gave everything else to my sister.

I called Ashley on my car phone. "Hey baby mama!"

"I'm headed to the hospital; my water broke while I was headed home."

She screamed. "I'm about to call my job, I'll be there tonight. Don't have my niece 'til I get there. Do you want me to call Christian?"

"Fuck no, I want to do this by myself or with you in there, but I can't wait on you."

"Sis, that's not fair."

"I don't care, I'll see you when you get here," I said and disconnected the call.

I drove at a normal speed and parked. "How can I help you today?"

"I think... I'm going into labor." That's all I remember before I looked down and saw blood coming from the bottom of my dress, and fainted.

Christian

"What up sis?" I asked Courtney. I was in the middle of handling something with a complication on the construction of an art gallery I was overseeing.

"Farren is in labor. The baby is in distress, and she's stressed; it's a few issues. The heartbeat isn't stable; just get here shit," she hung up the phone.

"Excuse me; I'll have my assistant come right over to record the meeting. My fiancé is in labor."

The Italians seemed pleased. "Congratulations, Mr. Knight. We will have to share a cigar when you return," they kissed my cheek. I slid into my Range Rover and did one-twenty all the way to River Oaks Hospital. I heard Farren screaming all the way down the hall. "How is she?" I asked my sister.

"If she would have listened months ago, she wouldn't be going through this and Ashley said she had took a second job working more than forty hours a week," she hissed.

"A second job for what?"

"If my niece doesn't make it, I'm going to slap that bitch. Who works two jobs when they're full term," she spat in anger. "Calm down; everything is going to be okay," I said trying to reassure us both. I had become a little nervous.

I scrubbed in, and came face to face with Farren for the first time since Christmas. "How are you doing?" I kissed her forehead, and pulled her hair out of her face.

"I just want this to be over," she said.

"You're doing so well," Ashley encouraged her, and fed her another ice chip.

She bent over and screamed. "Farren you are going to have to relax and breathe, and don't push," Courtney coached her.

"Please just take her out; I can't do this," she cried out in pain.

"Well if you weren't working and staying off your feet, we wouldn't be in this position," my sister snapped.

"Excuse me?" she looked.

"Courtney, chill," I told her.

"No Courtney, speak up. You got something you want to say" she asked.

Ashley said, "Look, now is not the time. Y'all both can leave and I'll go get another doctor."

"That's what I want," Farren said and leaned her head back.

"Yo ma, I don't care how you feel. I'm not missing the birth of my daughter," I told her.

"You sure she's yours? You know Dice is really still alive," she said with a smile. Ashley looked at her and so did Courtney.

"You got it." I held my jaw attempting to not go off on this dumb broad. Before I walked out the room I knocked everything off the carts.

"Chrissy," Courtney shouted after me.

"You know she was just pushing your buttons. How dare you walk out," she yelled and pushed me in the back. I turned around quickly. "Yo, fall back," I yelled.

I was so pissed I smoked a blunt in my car at the hospital. I've never in my life been so pissed. Where did we go wrong? I sat in my car for an hour or two just thinking about everything; her smile, our first argument, the way I used to hold her when we first met. She was so damn mean and I used to love that shit about her.

I was determined to make this right. I wanted my daughter coming to my home and no one else's. I was raised in a two-parent home, and my children would be the same way.

As I walked back to her room, I heard laughter and conversation. My entire family, along with Greg and a few of my potnas, all stood around Farren as she held my daughter.

Courtney came behind me and said, "I called your phone a million times. 7 pounds and 6 ounces," she smiled.

I dapped and hugged everybody, and kissed my mother on the cheek. Ashley was still crying.

I took my daughter from Farren's arms, and stared at her. A tear attempted to roll down my face. "Come on y'all, let's come back in the morning. Good job Farren," Chloe told everyone.

"Where's your key?" Ashley asked Farren. "Right there," she pointed.

"I'll be back later."

"She's beautiful," I whispered. "What's her name?"

"Carren Natalia Knight," she smiled.

"I love it," I said as I kissed my daughter. "I gotta get her some earrings," I told her.

She laughed. "You have to wait 'til she's three months."

"Daddy about to ice you out, boo," I told my daughter.

"Apologize for what you said earlier," I commanded her.

"No," she said.

"I know you didn't mean it, so just apologize and we can put this behind us," I said. I pulled a chair up to her bed and sat Carren in her bassinet.

"Why did you ruin my first Christmas with you?" she asked.

"Because I was about to propose to you and I had to make sure you were being one-hundred with me."

"Have I ever given you a reason to question me?" she asked.

"No," I told her.

"Okay then, so why now? I've done everything you ever asked me to do. I quit my favorite job, I'm home by eight, I'm cooking, fucking and sucking, and I've never done anything out the way. But you decide on Christmas Day to ask me if I set the love of my life up; that was a stab in my back," she told me.

"I don't know, Farren. I froze up man, I can't even explain it. I regret it every day, ma. I haven't been able to sleep...I need you with me," I confessed.

"Do you believe in your heart that I set him up? I can't sleep with you knowing you don't trust me," she asked.

I looked at her and held her hand in mine, as I kissed it. "I love you and I choose you; whatever you did in your past doesn't matter to me," I told her.

"You really don't believe me?" she looked surprised. It's not that I didn't believe my girl, it just looked a lil' fishy to me.

"It's not that, Farren," I told her. She pulled her hand back and turned her head.

I got up and kissed her forehead. "Just get some sleep; I'm right here when you wake up." She dozed off and so did I.

Before I knew it, Farren was asking where our daughter was. I quickly ensured her that she was okay, and the nurse took her down to run some more tests.

"They said you can leave in the morning, so Ashley will go to my house tonight to get it ready for you." Before she could protest, in walked some niggas I recognized from Hardy projects.

Farren

I couldn't believe I had given birth to a human being. My daughter had just become my motivation and inspiration for everything I planned on accomplishing in life. I had become a mother in a few short hours, and every second since she entered this world, I wanted her in my presence.

"What are y'all doing here?" I smiled.

The boys from the projects I grew up in, came in with balloons. "We saw Ashley at the gas station and she told us where you were. Why you ain't tell us you were even pregnant?" Pinto asked. I couldn't believe he was a man now; I literally had watched him grow up.

"Dominic just saw me. I'm surprised he ain't run back and say nothing," I told them.

Christian still sat there. "This is my boyfriend Christian. Christian, I grew up with these knuckleheads." He nodded his head and said he was going to check on Carren. He was such a mystery I couldn't tell how he was feeling.

"Yo, you a mama now," they all joked. It meant a lot to me that they all came to wish me well. They gave me a band full of money and made me promise I'll bring the baby to see all of their mamas and aunties.

Before I knew it, the doctor was coming in telling me I could prepare to go home. "You ready, ma?" Christian asked.

"You think if I set Dice up all of his workers would still be checking up on me, bringing me thousands of dollars for a baby I done had with another nigga from the other side of the tracks?" I asked him. As much as I didn't want to convince him I was loyal to Dice, it hurt me to know that he felt some type of way about me.

"I'm not on that anymore, Farren," he said.

"No, we need to squash this shit," I told him.

"I can't move in with you and continue life knowing you feel like I'm a traitor," I whined.

"I loved him with everything in me. Even when his daughters tried to jump me and his wife tried to get my mother fired from her job, I endured it all just to be with him. Everyone thought I was just some fast ass girl, but he loved me; Dice really fucked with me. I lost my world when I lost him, Christian. I was done with love. I gave up on niggas. I lived in a shell with no feelings," I confessed.

I remembered the night Dice took my virginity.

I went to prom with some local joker, but the real fireworks came when Dice picked me up from the high school gym in a rented Camaro. "You look beautiful, baby," he gleamed over me. He picked out my dress and told me how he wanted my hair, nails and everything.

"Thank you Dice," I blushed. I was nervous. I knew tonight was the night, and I was more than ready. We checked in at a hotel and he instructed me to get in the tub, and put on whatever was in in the shopping bag.

"I don't like lingerie," I joked. "I want you to wear that for me, baby." He patted me on the butt and

left the bathroom. I took my time moisturizing my body and making sure all my spots were clean and refreshed.

"Dice, where are you?" I asked. I had on a robe over the red bra and panty set. I was so nervous. I was seventeen and in a hotel with a thirty year old on my prom night. Most kids from prom were trying to sneak in the club, and I was about to get my back blown out for the first time.

"Come here; take that robe off," he instructed.

He was sitting on the couch rolling up a blunt. "Farren, I love your body," he smiled.

Before I knew it, he had me pent up on the wall, his head between my legs as my hands rested on his head, and I never in my life thought so much could pour from my inner love down to my ankles. Sweat bubbles rolled down my forehead. "Ohhh, ohhh...." I didn't know how to moan or what noises to make; I just knew he was making me feel so good.

"You going to cum in my mouth, baby?" he asked while he was still licking my pussy. "I think so," I whispered. He giggled and came up for air. "Girl, bring your young ass on." He picked me up and carried me to the bed. That night, I became a woman.

Snapping back into reality, I heard Christian asking me to lift my legs up so I could get out of the hospital bed and into my own bed. I missed my bed so much; the three-hundred count Egyptian sheets, fluffy pillows, and candles and wine. Hmm... I couldn't wait to have a drink.

Christian helped me to the wheelchair. "I love you and that's all that matters, and I'm still going to make you my wife and we're going to have more children." He kissed me on the forehead.

This argument wasn't over but for the sake of peace, I will let it go for now. The ride home was extremely quiet, and we were both lost in our own thoughts.

Christian meant the world to me; I just prayed that this rough patch wouldn't ruin us. He was the only man I wanted to be with. When I walked into the house with a slight limp, it was beautifully decorated with Christmas decorations and I smelled the aroma of food. "Welcome home baby," he whispered from behind me. Tears rolled down my eyes, and I saw that he redid the Christmas tree for me. There were so many gifts under the tree. I heard Boyz II Men playing in the background as Ashley took the baby and went upstairs.

"I love you, Farren. We started off right and we gon' be alright. Whatever shit we're dealing with, we're going to deal with it together. You are a mother now; your place is home and school. I don't want you working anymore." Before I could protest, he gave me a look and continued. "We're good. I love you; I don't care about what happened between you and Dice. You are my wife and the mother to my daughter. All I ever want in life is to make sure my family and home is taken care of. Will you do me the honor of taking my last name?" he asked, pulling a ring out his pocket.

I stood speechless and tear faced. Me, a girl from the projects, had escaped my reality and every statistic. "Yes," I nodded my head. He slid a five-carat, canary-yellow ring encrusted with diamonds around the band, on my finger. The ring was everything I could have ever imagined. He pulled me in for a hug and I could have sworn this man was crying. He held my chin. "This is forever Farren; no more walking out. You come to me with our problems," he instructed.

"Okay baby. I love you so much," I told him. I kissed him all over his face. We went to open all of my gifts and Christian definitely went all the way out. We ate dinner with Ashley and watched movies; Carren slept all through the night.

I woke up around eleven to my daughter screaming! I reached over to her crib. "It's okay mama, mommy is here," I cooed her. I decided to breastfeed my daughter. After feeding and burping her, I laid her back down. Christian was already gone for the day, and Ashley was in the kitchen fixing coffee. "Morning mommy," she smiled.

"Hi girl," I replied.

"How was last night?" she asked.

"Everything I didn't expect. I just wish I coulda gave him some, but we got five more weeks!" I joked.

"Did you see your other gift?" she asked.

"Girl, what else did that man get me? Ashley I don't need anything else," I told her.

"Go look outside," she smiled.

I walked to the front door, and a 2000 Range Rover fully loaded, black on black, sat in our driveway with a white bow. I peeped on the inside of the truck and saw a Louis Vuitton diaper bag that matched another bag which was for me. Christian had seriously outdone himself this year!

I texted him, "Thanks baby!!!!!!!!!!! I love you."

I posted a picture on Myspace and the caption read, "Still receiving gifts. Thanks bae!"

I was so blessed it was ridiculous. Within twenty minutes my sister was texting me, "What are you going to do with your BMW?"

"Merry Christmas to you, too, and Happy New Year. I'm fine and my daughter is fine; she's three days old. You haven't even asked about your niece, so don't ask me about my car!" I was so sick of my trifling family members.

"How long will you be here with me?" I asked my best friend and my daughter's godmother. "A few more days. I have a lot going on at work I need to get back to," she told me.

"I' m so happy you are here and I know Carren is, too," I told her. I limped back to the bed and took a nap; I couldn't wait to get my body back right. Christian was gon' hate it 'cause I would be living in the gym until I'm back to one-sixty.

Chapter 7

"Yo, you talked to my sister?" I asked Greg.

"Not in a minute. Why? Is everything good?"

"No it's not, she's pregnant," I told him.

"Damn, how long you knew?" he asked me surprisingly.

"A few months.... since around Thanksgiving," I told him, focusing on the pool game before me. He inhaled on the blunt a little longer.

"And it's mine, right?" he asked.

"She says it is," I answered his question.

He sat down at the bar in my basement, and I assumed we were done shooting pool. "Man, what the fuck!" he said.

"Chris, I don't know what to say. When was she going to tell me? What, she was gon' act like it was that nigga's kid or something?" he spat.

I shook my head. "I have no idea; y'all need to talk though. The only reason I stepped in was because apparently she wasn't going to say anything and it's an innocent child involved," I told my best friend.

He called her phone and she answered on the third ring. "Hi Greg, how are you?" She sounded happy.

"I'm at Christian's house; meet me here," he said and hung up the phone.

I started rolling up another blunt 'cause I knew he was gon' need it. An hour or so later, Courtney came downstairs. "Christian that baby is really yours," she said to me.

"I don't know how to take that, but nice to see you too, Courtney." I kissed her on the cheek and went upstairs to find my girl.

She was walking around, holding and singing to, Carren. "What did I do to your sister," she stopped and asked me.

"Why you ask me that?" I asked her.

"For one, she walked in my house and didn't speak, kissed my daughter and said she's really my brother's child. Christian, if you wanna get a DNA test, it's nothing; I'll pay for it myself," she shot.

"I know that's my daughter so chill out, and I'mma talk to my sister. She's been fly at the mouth for a minute. Give me my fat mama." I took my gun out of my pocket and slid it on the living room table while I cooed over my daughter. She had her mother's chink eyes, but her lips and nose were all daddy. Me and Farren were probably going to have about three or more kids; I wanted a house full.

I couldn't believe Carren was already three months; she was growing so fast. For July 4th, I wanted us to take our first trip as a family.

"I really want to take some summer courses." Farren sat by me and laid her head on my shoulder. "I thought you were going to focus on planning the wedding?" I asked her.

"I can do both. It's just May; school doesn't start until next month. I'm just taking two classes, going to the gym and planning the wedding." Farren was desperately trying to get back to her old body but I loved all the extra pounds.

"You don't need to lose no weight; I love all this," I said, slapping her thigh. She winced loudly in pain, causing Carren to turn in her sleep. "She's so spoiled," Farren stated.

"She gon' be spoiled her whole life, ain't that right mama?" I rubbed her head.

I heard Greg yelling. "What's going on down there? You need to go check," Farren said. I handed her the baby. "Go put my daughter to sleep, take a bubble bath and be playing with your pussy so when I get in there, I can just slide in." I looked her in the eyes, and she looked like she instantly went on fire.

"Give me a kiss," she commanded. I kissed her lips and she bit my tongue. "Oh, I got something for all that." I grabbed my dick to keep it down. Now it was operation 'get these niggas out my house'.

"You're going to leave your husband for me? I'm a street nigga! Is you fuckin crazy?" he yelled.

"It's getting late y'all," I told them. Courtney and her big belly looked stressed, confused and frustrated. I've seen it one too many times; women let their feelings get in the way of a good time.

"I'm out of here man, I'll holler at you." He looked at Courtney and walked over there. "Do what you gotta do. I care for you, but what you're thinking you going to get with me, you're not; I'm telling you now. I love the streets. I'm out every night, I got about three houses, I don't sleep in the same one two nights in a row, and I'm always out of town. I'm not the one Courtney," he told her, and he was telling the truth. Greg loved the nightlife. He loved the strip club. He wasn't a hoe in Philly from what I knew, but he traveled a lot so I wouldn't be surprised if he had a different girlfriend in every city. She looked away when he tried to touch her face. He dapped me up then dipped.

"I don't want to hear anything you gotta say; just go back to your perfect life," Courtney cried.

I bit my tongue. "I'm about to lock my house up," I said and went upstairs, waiting on her to get it together so I could meet my wife in the bedroom. She left with no explanation and I didn't bother to ask for one. Courtney was grown with three kids; she dug this hole her damn self.

I went to our bedroom and didn't find Farren. I searched the bathroom, and finally found her in the nursery with Carren, knocked out. I took our daughter and placed her in the crib. I woke Farren up. "Come on boo." She sleepily followed me to bed. I pulled the covers back and watched her sleep; she was so beautiful to me. Her wild hair blew up and down every time she inhaled and exhaled. Her lips poked out while she slept, but she looked happy and at peace. As long as I was living, she would always be happy; I made it my everyday mission. I kissed her forehead and joined her in rest.

"Bae, your phone keeps ringing," Farren kicked me. "Where is it?" I mumbled.

She got up, cut the light on and I heard her fumble for a bit. "HELLO," she answered in frustration. "Oh my God, are you serious? We're on the way." She looked at me with tears in her eyes; I immediately thought my daddy had died.

"Is my daddy okay?" I asked her.

"It's Courtney...she was in an accident by herself. Chloe thinks she tried to kill herself." She looked down as I exhaled. What the fuck was going on with my sister? Her actions were very selfish to me. If you aren't happy with your husband then divorce him. Don't take your life or your child's just to prove a point or to end your own misery.

"Stay here with Carren, I'll keep you posted," I told her. I slid on my basketball shorts and Nike slides.

"Now what do I look like being the only one not at the hospital?" she spat at me.

"Courtney and this stupid shit - man stay here," I instructed her to do so.

"No." She slid on the nearest dress on the floor and a cardigan. "I'll go get Carren's bag packed." It was no point in arguing with Farren.

I answered the car phone. "Ma I'm on the way," I said before she could get anything out.

"These kids up here scared as hell. What's wrong with Courtney? Who runs into a brick wall? And you know where she did this at, don't you?" she whispered. Farren looked over at me. "Where ma?" something was already telling me she was about to say Greg's house.

"Greg's; Christian, is your sister fooling around with that boy?" she asked.

"They got something going on, but that's not my business. How are the kids?" I changed the subject.

"Well Kennedy in here screaming her lungs out, the boys look sleepy and Courtney ole sorry ass husband talking about he has to be at work in three hours," mama fussed.

I yawned. "I'm pulling up in a minute, ma."

"Okay baby," she said.

"Your sister is fuckin Greg?" Farren asked.

"Yep." I turned the radio up just a lil'; not too loud to wake my daughter up.

The hospital was a mess. Greg was in a corner, Courtney's husband, Derrick, sat in another corner scanning his cellphone, my daddy and my mama kept dozing off, and Farren was coaxing Kennedy to fall asleep, but she had a million and one questions.

"Y'all can go on home. Your sister will be okay; however, she has lost the baby. It was a boy. The psychiatrist is going to have some questions for the immediate family," Farren's sister told me. I was thankful for her working the night shift. She could've lost her job delivering us that information; but in Philly, doctors took forever to come and talk to the family.

I looked over at Greg. As much as he hung out, I knew it had to pain him to hear he was having a son.

"You should go see your niece. I think she's up now." I smiled at Neeki, and pointed her into Farren's direction.

"Come on boys; mommy is okay. Let's get y'all home and dressed for camp," Courtney's husband, Derrick instructed.

"You just lost a child and you have nothing to say?" Chloe asked.

My mother stepped in, "Chloe, be quiet."

He looked at Chloe. "A child that wasn't mine. I haven't touched Courtney in almost two years; we don't even sleep in the same room. That baby wasn't mine, so what do you expect me to feel? The only reason I came here was for my children." Courtney's husband wasn't always an asshole. I'm starting to think their problems were all my sister's fault.

"Don't you dare lie on my sister in front of her own kids," Chloe yelled.

"Chloe shut up, okay. Just shut up. You don't even know what you're talking about," I told her. She looked at me. "Oh, I forgot you and Courtney and all y'all secrets. I'm out of here." She grabbed her keys and left. My sister was a goody two shoes; always knew it all. I loved her wholeheartedly, but fucked with her from a distance.

"Ma, I'm tired; I have to be to work in less than four hours. I'm not staying up here," I told her once we were the only ones left, in addition to Greg. Chloe had taken my daddy back home.

"You know I'm not leaving my child up here, crazy or not, Chrissy. I'll be here when she wakes up," she said worriedly.

"Gregory, you can go home, baby," my mama told Greg. He looked confused and shocked. "I'mma stay Mrs. Knight," he told her.

"I'll be back up here. You need something?" I asked my mother. "No. Farren this baby is getting heavy! How many times a day are you breastfeeding?" she asked.

"All day; I didn't know I could breastfeed and feed her other milk." she stated shocked.

"Ohh baby, when it's time for you to go back to school, this baby gon' have a fit." She placed Carren in her car seat.

"Beautiful baby, sis," Nikki beamed in the car seat. "Thanks," she replied.

"Ma, I'm out of here. Aye my brother, hit my line later," I told Greg. I knew we couldn't talk right now with my mama up here.

Once we arrived back at our home, the sun was out. "I might as well get dressed," I told Farren.

"Yep. I'm about to get Carren back to bed and go to sleep. I'm still sleepy," she said.

I stretched my arms, debating if I wanted to do the same. "I got too much to do today," I told myself.

"Let me get up outta here," I stated to no one in particular. I joined Farren in the shower; we both smelled like a hospital.

"When you gon' give me some more babies?" I asked as I washed her back. "After law school, Christian. You keep asking me that and I'mma get on some birth control," she stated.

"Do what you gotta do, boo. Just know I want about four more." I slid the washcloth between her legs.

"Oh really?" she asked.

"Yep," I told her. I rinsed and dried the both of us off, and while she slipped back in between our Egyptian sheets, I was getting dressed in black slacks, a blue button down and added my Cartier cufflinks.

"I love you. Call me when you wake up." I kissed her on the forehead. "Cut the alarm on," she said back.

Greg called me, as if on cue, as soon as I got in the car. "What up sir," I answered my ringing phone.

"Mannnnnnnnnnnnnnnnnn, what the fuck bruh," he yelled.

I took a deep breath. "I'm feeling the same you way are right now."

"Chris, man I don't do nut cases; that's some lunatic type shit. She done tore my damn house up," he fussed.

"Yeah, the damage is gon' take a minute to replace. I'll send someone out there," I offered.

"I just stared at her. Did you think this would make me fuck with you more or something?" It seemed as if he asked the questions to himself, but wanted answers instantly. I said nothing.

"That shit is crazy. Let me know when you come from up there," I told him.

"I'm already gone; her ass ain't have shit to say," he told me.

"Damn man. Well let me make some calls and I'll rap with you later," was my last reply before I disconnected the call.

Courtney was too grown and too successful to have these types of problems like a lovesick teenager. But I guess love made you do crazy things, or so I have heard.

I spent the day tying up loose ends and endless meetings. My business was booming since the opening of Harold's, and it seemed as if every chef was requesting blueprints to design their dream kitchen and restaurant. I couldn't be more ecstatic.

"I'm so horny. When will you be home?" my fiancé texted me.

"Late boo. Stay up though, daddy got you," I instantly replied. I loved how I was responsible for bringing out Farren's freak side; her body always yearned for mine.

"Okay baby," she wrote back.

The pile on top of my desk seemed to never end, and the clock had already struck midnight.

Farren

As soon as I heard the door click and the alarm silence, I was relieved that my daughter had just fallen asleep. I slid off of my t-shirt and went down the steps with nothing on at all. Christian was taking his loafers off at the front door and loosening his tie.

"How was work?" I asked. He turned his head, and his lips formed a sly smile. I'm sure daddy wasn't expecting all of this after a long day of work. He undressed as he headed towards me, dropping items of clothing with each step he took. On the stairs around four in the morning, is when his lips met mine, and it seemed as if it had been hours since our last time making love when in fact it was a few days; but every day I desired his touch.

Even when he wasn't by my side, my pussy pulsated as if he was inside of me. It's safe to say I was obsessed with my man. I prayed for him more than I prayed for myself. He was literally my every breath. I enjoyed his touch; it made me tingle and shiver internally and externally. He kissed my lips, ears and nose. "Ohhhh," I moaned out. I wrapped my arms around his neck and held on, because I knew it was about to be a very long night.

"Missed me?" he asked, breathing hard, whimpering in my ear, dick rubbing against my slit, daring not to enter me. Christian was going to brain fuck me before he did physically.

"Yes Daddy." I pushed him back and opened my legs. He slid down a few steps and cut the light on over the stairway. "Why you stop? Did I tell you to stop? Keep playing with my pussy," he instructed me. His tone was raspy because he had a long day, probably full of conference calls and meetings.

I nodded my head and obeyed my future husband. I licked my finger and toiled with my nipples, and slid those same wet fingers inside of my pussy. I immediately creamed and poured. It was so quiet that you could hear me swirl around my vagina, because I was so damn wet.

"How do you feel right now, Farren?" he asked. He stood over me watching me play with my pussy, making love to it wishing it was him.

"I feel good baby..... uh, ohhhhh, yessssssssssssssssssss," I yelled. I brought myself to an orgasm and attempted to catch my breath and come down off of my own personal high.

"Farren baby, can I taste you?" he asked. Christian was always playing mind games with me; he liked to see me weak before he entered me. I couldn't answer. I held my head back, body heaving up and down. I was exhausted off of foreplay.

He didn't wait for an answer. He kneeled before, parted my legs once more, placed two fingers inside my hole and his thumb in my ass; not all the way, but enough for me to feel pressure coming from two holes. I attempted to hold on for the ride. "Hmmmm," I hummed. I ground my hips with the rhythm of his fingers.

"Baby....shit baby, come on baby," he talked and licked. "Mother fuckin' pussy tastes so damn good," he talked and sucked. "Come on ma, give me some more of that pussy; open them legs up," he talked and bit down on my clit.

"Christiannnnnnnnnnnnnnnnn," I moaned, and for the first time I think I squirted. It went everywhere. Christian looked up at me and his eyes bucked; I knew this nigga was feeling like the man of the year now!

"Bring your pretty ass on up here. You know you about to get it." He turned me over and smacked me on the ass. We didn't even make it all the way up the steps before he was ready to get up in me.

Placing his hands on the middle of my back, he commanded that I get low and bring my ass up high. "Stay down," he whispered in my ear. He ran his tongue gently down my spine and I exhaled slowly. Christian was about to tear me up and I twerked, which he already knew I was more than ready for the punishment.

"Hmmm..... twerk on this dick baby." He smacked my ass as he entered me slowly. I tightened my walls as he went back in. Those nine inches of heaven made me cream instantly; I heard and felt it.

"Get it Christian." I fought back, throwing my ass in a circle, up and down on his dick. He made me feel so complete in and out, that a tear ran down my face. I didn't know fucking could feel like making love. Before I could climax once more, Carren burst out crying.

"Stay right here; don't move," he told me. I watched my naked baby daddy wash his hands in the guest bathroom, dick still hard as a brick, and go tend to our baby.

"Farren, bring a bottle," he yelled. My legs felt like cold pasta. Somehow I managed to get an already made bottle out of the fridge and heat it up. I walked into our daughter's nursery and handed it to him. In no time, Carren was back asleep.

In our master bedroom, I was looking for my panties to place them back on. I bent over to pick them up and Christian had taken hold of my hips and thrust his dick into me. "Christian." I laughed. "Come on," he pumped slowly.

"I'm through with you tonight. It's almost 6 a.m., boy," I yelled.

He held me from behind, dick still inside and all, and led me to the bed. "Mmmm," I moaned with my leg draped over his shoulder.

"Come on bae." He stroked my clit and made love to me so gentle and passionately.

"I love you so much, Christian," I whispered. I was so set. My vagina made a love song all on its own; music was not needed.

"I love you more baby," he told me. We went at it for hours and hours and hours. The sun had rose and settled before we ended. I knew I would be in bed all day; Christian had a way of sending me into a deep sleep. My only prayer was that Carren would be at peace today.

"Let's go out to dinner tonight; you don't have to cook," Christian said to me. We were just getting up and out the bed around 5 p.m. We had lazily lounged around the house since about noon.

I loved days like this; I, he and Carren making memories that will last forever.

"Are you sure? You know I don't mind cooking," I asked. I enjoyed being at home with my daughter every day. I would soon be back into the normal swing of things once school returns.

"Yeah. I want to see you dressed up in heels and shit," he told me not looking up, because he was carefully watching Carren in her swing that he didn't trust at all. He hated the automated swing while I thought it was a complete life saver.

"Okay boo. Let me start on my hair now so we can be out of here by 8." I got up and headed to the bathroom to press my long mane, which took an hour and a half. We had bathed prior to watching movies, so I slipped on my favorite Express jeans that fit me like a leather glove in the wintertime and a hot pink shirt with gold bows on the collar. My shoes are what set the outfit off. They were "thank you gifts" from Christian a few months ago; the black platform Giuseppe shoe with a hot pink sole that I adored. I added my rose-gold Rolex watch and rose-gold Cartier diamond earrings, and sprayed a few dashes of Jo Malone on my wrist and behind my ear.

"Look at your mommy," Christian beamed at me while he had our daughter making sweet faces at me. He ushered me and Carren into the Mercedes. We rarely drove this car; Christian and I both adored our Ranges.

"Where you wanna eat?" he asked as we headed into the city. "It doesn't matter boo, whatever you want. I think I'm just kind of happy to be out the house," I laughed.

"I told you that we have to remember to live, and you're gon' start getting out more. You can't just wait till Ashley comes to visit," my fiancé told me. He had one hand on the steering wheel and the other on my thigh.

"I want some steak," he said. "That sounds good to me, baby." We took the highway to

Dantanna's, a popular steakhouse in Philadelphia.

"Christian," we heard a voice approach our table. I saw Christian clench the inside of his jaw, and I wondered who the woman was. Lord knows I didn't feel like dealing with no bullshit today.

"How are you?" he asked. I took a sip of my wine and attempted to look as comfortable as I could fathom.

She came closer. I looked her over as I sat the glass of Dantanna's finest wine back on the white linen that was placed horizontally across the dinner table. She was tall... almost as tall as Christian. Her skin was dark... almost as dark as Christian's. And she wore the longest weave I've ever seen in my life. I studied her hips briefly, and if she was a fling of the past, it was her ass that drawn Christian to her, not her face.

I wasn't an envious woman; I was confident in my appearance. I enjoyed makeup but it didn't make me the woman I am today. I rarely wore weave because my hair was naturally curly, but I did have to work out constantly to keep a certain weight because I wasn't born skinny. But looking over at this woman, I knew instantly that she had to fight to keep Christian, because off of her looks alone, she definitely didn't have him.

"I'm well. What are you doing here?" she asked. Her bebe dress did her body justice; I will give the young woman her props, even though she appeared to be way older than me.

"Having dinner with my fiancé; this is Farren and our daughter, Carren," he introduced me. I smiled, "Nice to meet you."

"I'm Miranda, Christian's fiancé from last year. I see you got her a new ring. Well can I have mines back?" she asked as an attempt to make a joke.

He sipped his Hennessy. "Enjoy the rest of your night," he dismissed her.

"Likewise." She waltzed off.

"That's your old bae?" I smirked. "Shut up girl." He flashed those pearly whites that I loved so much.

"Do you have a type?" I asked him.

"Yep, you, so next subject."

I ate a piece of the cheesecake that we shared. "No, really baby. Like for me, I like light-skinned guys, but you're dark skin. You're normally not my type, but I was attracted to you anyway," I told him.

"Were you really? It took us so long to have sex," he admitted.

I smiled at him. "Was it worth the wait?"

He nodded his head and returned the smile. "Well worth it," he told me.

"What do you want to do for your birthday?" he asked again.

"Nothing. I'm studying for these summer finals," I told him.

"Nah babe, we're doing something. Anywhere you wanna go?" he asked.

"Nope." I picked up Carren and played with her.

"You're so difficult," he muttered.

"No, I'm so simple and that bothers you," I replied. Christian wanted me to be this flamboyant female that I wasn't, and at times I wish he would just accept that I enjoyed being home with our daughter. I looked forward to the simple things like making his meals. I liked our life; I didn't need the trips and all that other bullshit.

"Let's go. I want some more of you before I go to sleep." He placed two hundred-dollar bills on the table, which were enough to cover the tab and tip. Christian placed his hat on his head, grabbed Carren's car seat and ushered me to the valet booth.

"She's beautiful," someone said as they peered over my shoulder, looking at my daughter.

I turned around to say thank you and didn't see a face or a person. Either I was going crazy or something wasn't right. I moved closer to Christian and waited impatiently for our car to come around.

Once we were in the car, Christian took a phone call after ignoring his ringing phone throughout dinner.

"What man? Nah, I'm not going to be able to make it," Christian told whoever called him once we were en route to the house. "I got my girl with me," he told them. "No, what the fuck I look like. Are you stupid?" he yelled.

Carren erupted into tears and I turned over to coo her. "Daddy didn't mean to scare you, princess" I told my daughter. "It's okay pookie, it's okay." I shook her finger and rubbed her stomach. I slid over to the side of the car and hit my head on the window. "Christian, slow down, what is wrong with you?" I asked him.

"Can you shoot a gun?" he asked.

"Yeah, why?" I asked.

He rolled down the window. "Shoot at that black Impala," he told me.

"What the fuck! My daughter is in the car," I yelled at him.

He threw me a gun. "Shut the fuck up right now. You don't think I know that? Shoot!" I huffed and slid down in my seat. I saw the car getting closer. I shot one bullet into the window, and another at the tire, then another at another tire. No one shot back... no one did anything.

Other cars were honking at us and a whole bunch of other crazy stuff. Christian turned down a few back streets, and I prayed that no one wrote his tag number down.

"Damn baby," he said when we pulled up at a nice brownstone in a suburban area.

"What nigga?" I asked trying to calm down a screaming Carren.

"You just turned me on." He looked at me through the rearview mirror with pure lust in his eyes. How can your dick be hard when our life could have ended in a few short moments?

"We gon' have to talk. Where are we?" I asked. The neighborhood was quiet, and the house sat cozily in the cul-de-sac.

"My other house; we need to switch cars," he told me. He pulled the car around the side of the house, and quickly we switched to an older dark blue Lexus.

He didn't say anything for a long time. He spoke quietly on the phone as I sat in the back seat with my daughter, rocking her car seat to keep her as peaceful as possible.

We were driving so long, I fell asleep. What was supposed to be a beautiful romantic night had turned out to be the complete opposite. I woke up and the sun was out. I was in the back seat of the car knocked out. The doors were locked and there was no Christian; all I saw was a bridge and men standing ahead. I grabbed the .9 at my feet, and got out the car with the gun at my side.

They must have heard my heels clicking against the pavement, because everyone turned around. "Babe put that gun down, what are you doing? Why do you have a gun?" Christian walked over to me. Greg and a few other men I noticed all looked at me and laughed.

"Damn Farren, it's like that? You was gon' shoot me" Greg joked. I didn't find a damn thing funny.

"Where the fuck are we? You gon' let your family sleep in the car while you chop it up with your niggas?" I asked. I could have spazzed but from being with Dice, I knew to never embarrass your man or yourself in front of anyone, it didn't matter who you were around. Home business is home business.

"I didn't want or have time to take you home; I wanted you near me." He kissed my forehead.

"Okay, well can we go?" I asked. I wanted to bathe and get in the bed, not be standing outside on no damn abandoned bridge.

"Yes baby, whatever you want. It was an emergency meeting; I had to handle some shit. Go get in the car, here I come." He patted my behind and sent me on my way. Whatever Christian said is usually what went.

As I "patiently" waited on my fiancé to wrap up his business, I remembered the first time I ever saw Dice get into some shit.

We were chilling at his cousin's house, and someone knocked on the door. "Bae get the door," he yelled at me. He was counting up some money. I walked to the door, and as soon as I opened it, Dice's little cousin fell into my arms; teeth missing, eye busted, and his clothes were drowning in blood. "DICE," I screamed. Instantly tears poured out of my eyes, because I knew lil' Peanut; I knew him my whole life, and I feared if he would make it through the night.

"What's wrong bae?" he yelled.

"Put that fuckin money down and help me," I yelled again.

He ran in there, *"who the fuck you...,"* before he could complete his fuss, he looked down at me on the floor with his cousin's body in my hands.

He choked on his blood. *"They caught me cuz,"* he mumbled.

"Stop talking. Dice, call the police, call somebody," I yelled.

He kneeled over me. *"Who did this Nut, tell me?"* he asked.

"I don't know man," he managed to get out.

"Don't let me die," he begged.

Dice went and got his phone, and thirty minutes later some nurse bitch came and did all she could, but begged Dice to let her take him to the doctor. *"Nah, cops know your scandalous ass. My girl gon' have to go,"* I heard him say in the kitchen.

"She doesn't even have a car," I heard her huff.

"Yo shut the fuck up, I'm thinking," Dice yelled at her. Before I knew it, I heard his Timberlands enter the living room. "What you need me to do?" I asked without looking up.

"Take Nut to the ER and say he was your boyfriend. Baby you know what to do," he told me.

"Okay, give me your keys," I said and got up. I hated to lie. I hated to even be placed in this situation, but I loved my boyfriend with everything in me, even though he really wasn't my boyfriend. He was a thirty-year-old man with four children, and I was a seventeen-year-old girl that only saw her daddy on holidays. I was looking for love in all the wrong places.

Chapter 8

Christian was so busy the next two weeks, I barely saw him. For him to be so "excited" for my birthday, I didn't even see him the night before, and I just knew I would wake up to him on my twenty-seventh birthday. I was born July 4th, but I didn't feel any fireworks or celebration. My fiancé came home every two or three days with blood all over his clothes. They were so soiled that half of the time I would just throw them away. He was too busy to do anything but sleep. His phone would be ringing off the hook to the point where he only got two to three hours of rest.

I knew he was neglecting his "real" business, the one he fought so hard to obtain. His parents always called the house asking why we haven't been to Sunday dinner. Christian forbade me to leave the house. We were staying at his other home which was so deep in the country I had to take an extended vacation from work, and have my classes switched to online. I barely talked to him; not that we were arguing, it was just whatever the fuck happened that night from that car following us, seriously had my fiancé shaken up.

I scanned through my text messages from people I barely spoke to, wishing me a Happy Birthday, and even on Myspace. I barely returned calls. All I really wanted on this day was to spend it with my fiancé and my daughter. I called Christian phone around eleven and he didn't answer. I decided at that moment that I wasn't spending my birthday in bed, and I didn't care what he would say.

I dressed my daughter in a Burberry dress and Burberry baby booties, and I slipped a Donna Karen tangerine one-piece jumpsuit with my beige Bally sandals. Me and Carren enjoyed ourselves at a nail salon I found not too far from the house, and we had lunch at Maggiano's. I stopped and got myself some flowers, fresh lamb chops, two movies from Redbox, and a fifth of Patron.

Carren looked happy to be spending my birthday with me. Around 4 p.m., I finally got the strength to return a few calls, and then started on dinner. A few more hours passed before I sat at the table alone, eating lamb and squash. The alarm chimed and in walked my fiancé a few short minutes before my birthday came to an end. He came in with balloons, roses and a bag with the label Celine on it.

What Christian continuously failed to realize about me was it wasn't the gifts that impressed me or kept me; it was the time and attention he gave me. A woman will leave a man faster for not spending time with her than lack of what he brings to the table.

I was always biting my tongue to keep him happy, and to avoid arguments and keep the peace in our home, but tonight it wasn't happening. I didn't give a damn if those roses were freshly picked, my birthday is a special day to me and all I requested of him was his time.

"Did you not get my message?" I shot.

He placed everything on the kitchen island. "What message baby?" he asked, sticking his finger in the pot that held the special garlic parmesan pasta.

"All I want to do on my birthday is spend time with you and Carren. I sent that four days ago which is also the last time I seen or heard from you," I yelled.

"I'm here now Farren. Happy Birthday, baby. I love you. I'm here now," he tried to sooth me. "Check the clock. It's no longer my fuckin' birthday, and you can take this purse back, I already have it." I kicked the bag on the floor, and went to my room.

It was literally nothing he could say to me at this point. I never asked for anything and never requested much, but his time. That's all I ever wanted was his time, and lately I didn't even receive that.

"Farren, you know what's going on so why are you tripping," he said when he walked in the room.

"And you know it's my birthday so why are *you* tripping? It apparently didn't mean that much to you. You put absolutely no thought into this gift because if you would have, you would've known I already had that purse," I told him.

"I will take the purse back and you can get whatever bag you want, boo," he told me. He didn't even attempt to make me feel any better.

"It's not about the bag. I don't care about no damn purse. It's your time; it's you spending time with me and your daughter, calling and texting. I didn't fall in love or move in with you because of the gifts. And you promised me in the beginning that this wasn't your life; all you did was collect money. I don't like feeling like I'm going to lose you. I did not sign up for this," I admitted.

"I don't get involved but when my life is threatened, I'm all in 'til the shit is nipped in the bud. We will have plenty of time to celebrate your birthday." He stripped out of his clothes.

"You're still missing my point... it's cool." I pulled back the comforter and prepared for bed.

"Come shower with me," he called from the bathroom. I completely ignored his ass and went to sleep.

Christian

I loved my boo; she didn't bitch about anything. She cooked every night and wasn't big on shopping, but when she did go, she enjoyed herself. My family loved her and she was a great mother; smart, ambitious, successful, loving, caring and very supportive. Farren meant the world to me and I would do anything in my power to ensure that I would always have her. It was a lot of unnecessary bullshit going on in my inner circle and that's what bothered me; it bothered me a lot.

I was keeping late nights because we were staking out different locations, trying to see who wasn't being loyal. It had gotten to a point where niggas started sleeping on me, because I fell back and put more time to go legit and clean; but right when they thought I would never step back on the streets, they were in for a rude awakening. My trigger finger had become super itchy, and we were knocking niggas off left and right.

I didn't forget Farren's birthday, but today's timing was very bad and I didn't like using my phone too much these days. It pained me to see my daddy calling to talk to me about the game or the news, and I had to send him to ignore because I was in the middle of a riot or bustin' somebody's head open.

After I dried off and threw on some boxers, I went to check on my daughter and she was knocked out; slobbing and all. Carren slept just like her mama.

I slid in the bed and held my future wife. "Daddy loves you and when all this shit blows over, we're going to London to get married; just you and me, and work on baby number 2." I kissed her cheek.

"When you start spending more time with baby number one, then just *maybe* I will consider baby number two. Right now, get off me," she hissed.

I was planning on fucking her, but her mouth was just too hot for me. I rolled over and went to sleep on her ass.

The next morning I heard Carren crying and Farren trying to get her back to sleep. Soon after she entered the room, I greeted her, "Good morning." She shot a smirk in my direction. "I'm going to Atlanta for the weekend. I already asked Chloe to watch Carren," she told me while she pulled out her MCM suitcase.

"I think you need to wait until I can go with you." Farren was attempting to be ignorant, but the only thing that I was concerned with was our family's safety.

"I don't need you to go with me, I'm good. I'm just going to get a peace of mind and to drink and enjoy my birthday," she replied. It was so obvious she was still mad about her birthday. She did nothing to disguise her attitude and bitter display of affection.

"I'll let you learn on your own. Enjoy yourself." I gave up. If something happened, I would be the one to deal with it.

I dropped her off at the airport. "Do you have enough money? Here's my card; call me time the plane lands." I handed her my card and a few hundred dollars.

"Thanks, but I'm good." She left the money and card on the console. She turned around and kissed Carren. "Mommy will be back soon, princess. Be good for your auntie," she cooed.

I leaned over to kiss her cheek, and she opened the door and dipped.

"Why is your mama so crazy, Carren." I shook my head and laughed.

Things change like the seasons do

Present Day

"We tend to ignore the signs and wonders, when they're usually right in front of our face."

"Ms. Walters, glad you could join us." Nick Connor, head of the DEA, stood up and shook Farren's hand as she walked into a meeting she was completely unprepared for and knew absolutely nothing about. "I would say thank you, but I'm unsure of what this meeting is about," Farren replied. She did not believe in beating around the bush, or playing games.

Farren was confident in her work; she knew she performed well and always crossed her t's and dotted her i's. If an error was made or there was a loophole in any of her cases, she would be extremely disappointed in herself. For the past ten years, she worked her way up the legal ladder, working her ass off to be the best attorney she could be. She always stayed the extra hours, grinded way past the midnight hour, was the first to enter the office and the last to leave.

She was never certain whether it was the color of her skin or the fact that the money she made off of cases simply went to charities and nonprofits she supported around the cities of Philadelphia and New York. Farren did not socialize in the office, did not believe in catching a drink after a long day of depositions, or even popping champagne after she won cases that were worth millions of dollars. She took her lunch at the same time every day and never invited anyone to go with her. Farren handled her business and she handled it well. She was the mother of three beautiful children and the proud wife to Christian Knight. "Have a seat, let's chat. How is your family?" Another person asked.

Farren's head snapped back. "Cut to the bullshit, if you wanted to hire me you would have contacted my office, so how can I help you, sir?" Farren sat her Celine purse, iPhone and Blackberry on the counter, and tapped her perfectly manicured fingernails on the wooden table. Her ten-carat wedding ring and Cartier band glimmered, which was a "just because gift" from her husband and best friend of fifteen years. Before she even entered the room, her Bond fragrance and Dior pumps, clicking and clacking against the tiled floor, warned the federal agents that Mrs. Knight had entered the building.

At forty years old, she worked hard as hell as a commercial attorney at one of the top firms in New York. She drove an hour and a half to work every day, waking up at 5 a.m. to run with her husband and see her children off to school. Farren was a proud soccer mom, Girl Scout volunteer, and a very active Delta in her local graduate chapter; she was a woman who wore many hats. She did not waste time on nothingness. In her life, every second of the day was cherished and important to her.

One folder was placed in front of her. "How about you open this and you tell us what we need to know, and you just might make it home before dinner to feed Carren, Michael, and Noel," the agent smirked at her. Farren was shocked, but her face remained stone. She knew the game and she knew it well. As bad as these men probably wanted to see her crack, they would not.

She picked up the folder, stood to her feet, closed her suit jacket and simply said, "As soon as I review these documents, I will give you a call."

"We need to talk to you today," the agent stated. "Let her go, she will be calling soon. I know her kind," the boss said in a matter-of-fact tone. Farren offered a warm smile, and walked coolly to her Range Rover. She could barely get in her car and out of the parking lot fast enough; her hands were shaking and she was beginning to panic. With the swipe of her finger, she unlocked her phone and dialed "Hubby" in her favorites. "Babe, you're calling early? You must want some more from this morning," her husband said jokingly upon answering the phone, only today there was nothing to laugh about.

"Baby, I can't talk over the phone, just tell me where you are," Farren yelled.

"What's wrong, Farren?" Christian asked. He was always concerned with his family's well-being.

"I can't talk over the phone, where the fuck are you?" she asked. Her line clicked, informing her that her assistant was calling.

"My office; slow down because I know you're speeding." He disconnected the call as Farren clicked over. "Farren Knight," she answered. Even in the midst of everything she knew she was soon to face, she still had to remain corporate.

"Some roses came for you, Mrs. Knight," her assistant, Dolly, reported cheerfully. "I won't be in today, sweetie, just put them on my desk. Can you handle everything today? I don't want any calls or emails unless it's an emergency," Farren stated. She already knew Dolly wouldn't mind. Because of Farren, Dolly was able to take care of her two young daughters, live in a gated neighborhood and attend school. "Yes ma'am." Dolly knew not to ask any questions, just to do as Farren said. Farren did not tell her enough how much she appreciated her and looked to her as a daughter, or even younger sister.

Farren pulled up to her husband's office and took the elevator to the seventh floor where she was greeted by his receptionist. She knew she was probably giving Christian head from time to time, but today she wasn't in the mood to roll her eyes and toss her neck; she needed to see her husband. Christian looked as if he was waiting on her to get there. She slammed the door and threw the folder on his desk.

"What the fuck have you been doing!" she yelled with tears in her eyes and mascara running down her face. She snatched her Prada shades off so fast, the handle broke. Christian saw the anger in her eyes; it was mixed in with fear.

He sat down and reviewed the contents. This information only had to come from a rat; there was a rat in his camp. He leaned back in his Italian leather chair and rubbed his hand over his face, after twenty minutes or so of complete silence.

"Christian, my career is on the line. Our kids? They know our kids names and named them one by one," Farren panicked.

"They fuckin' what? They what?" His eyeballs damn near popped out of his head as his fingers scrambled around the keyboard.

"I can't believe this shit right now," she cried into his arms. He stared at the documents wishing the information was assigned to another person; not him, nor his wife, nor his kids. His mother...his sisters... if his father was still living he also, would be so disappointed in him.

A young guy walked in Christian's office. "You have one hour to find out who the fuck is talking, and you have three days to have someone handle this motherfuckin' situation. My wife's life should be back to normal by Monday. MONDAY. You see her face, huh stupid ass nigga. Do you see her face? She's crying. I don't make my wife cry, I make her smile and cum. You see that frown? I can't go to sleep knowing that's how she feels. You wanted to be in charge, so you better fix this shit, NOW!" Christian banged his fist on his desk as he barked orders and threats to the guy he left in charge.

He didn't tell his wife any lies; he had left that life a few years ago. Now he was the daddy of the year. He didn't miss dance recitals, soccer or football games; he never missed Sunday dinners, he fucked his wife five times a week and made sure everyone in his family was well taken care of. This was not a part of his retirement plan. Christian would be fifty in September; this was not how he planned on starting his summer, in court for some shit he didn't do.

He hated people who were sloppy handling business. Christian paid people to get their hands dirty. He didn't move, touch or see the work. He stopped collecting money on drugs a long time ago. Christian made more than enough money in his legit businesses. He was a role model in his community and in his home, and his children went to a prestigious private school. How embarrassing would it be if the other parents saw cool, laidback Mr. Knight getting arrested for some bullshit money laundering and drug charges? It was beneath his caliber.

"I'm on it boss." The young man tipped his hat and exited as quietly as he entered.

Christian went to his wife's side and held her in his arms. Her arms were placed highly on the window overlooking downtown Philadelphia, as she breathed in and out. "I'm not blaming you baby; anything you need me to do I will do it," she admitted.

Farren loved her husband. It was true that he was all the family she had outside of her children and best friend. She hadn't communicated with her mother and sister in years. Her father was amazing, but their lack of communication had been existent for years; too long for her to even care to fix the problem, so she loved him from a distance. Farren ate, lived and breathed her husband. She balanced her life off of his; he was really her everything. She fell in love with him more and more every day. He meant the world to her. Even years later after the wedding bells died and the horses went to sleep, she still basked in his presence, still got high off his aroma; even their lovemaking felt new every single time.

"Nothing is going to happen, and you're good baby," he whispered in her ear. His arms left her waist and somehow slipped in between her legs. "How do you taste?" he asked. She turned to look at him. "Turn back around Farren. Look ahead. Take your mind off of everything today; let me fuck you." He moaned and licked her neck and ear. She exhaled when she felt her husband's fingers enter her honeycomb. She felt him in her soul and before she knew it, she silently came all over his hand.

"How do you taste, Farren?" Christian asked her again. She took his fingers in her hand and licked each and every single one.

He dropped his Valentino pants to the floor, and slowly but surely brought her peace and happiness, as he rocked gently inside of her. His dick brought her back down to earth, but his strokes took her to heaven. Farren felt like she was high off of a pill. "Yessssssss." This was nothing new for the married couple; they made love and fucked when and wherever they wanted to, no matter the location.

"Baby, why is this pussy always so wet and tight, shit!" Christian complimented Farren. He decided to speed up his thrusts since they were at his place of business.

"Because it's yours daddy." She bent all the way over, grabbed her ankles, and popped

on her husband's dick, giving him an open view
of everything he needed to see to climax. He bit
the inside of his mouth, took a deep breath, and
smacked her ass gently; not too loud to disturb
his employees or staff. "Hmmmmmmmmmmmm
Christian, please cum with me; baby cum with
me," Farren moaned. Christian took control of
the game they played with each other. He
grabbed her ass and dipped in her pussy once,
twice, and three more times, before they both
were overcome with joy and much pleasure.
After cleaning each other up, Farren looked
brand new as if her husband wouldn't be soon
indicted on charges such as money laundering,
intent to distribute, distribution, conspiracy to
distribute, murder, kidnapping, and the rap
sheet had more explicit details.

"I think I'm going to get my kids early, and
take them shopping," Farren told her husband.
"I'mma go with you; I don't want you out by

yourself." He prepared to end his day early, forwarding calls to his cell phone and such.

The couple exited the office ignoring the few stares and shocked faces of his staff, especially the young and dumb receptionist. Farren winked at her before the elevator doors closed. "Your girlfriend is mad," she commented.

He texted on his phone, not daring to make eye contact with his wife. "What are you talking about, boo?" he asked.

"Nothing at all Christian. We might as well drop my car off at the house," Farren advised.

After hopping in her husband's Porsche truck, picking up the children from school, and spending the entire day as a family, Farren was exhausted.

"I'm so tired and I know I have tons of work to do tomorrow," Farren whined to her husband. "Mommy, do we have to go to school tomorrow?" Farren's youngest daughter asked. They were all in their parents' bedroom watching a movie. Noel laid in between her mother's legs. Both of her daughters inherited her wild and fuzzy hair, and Noel preferred to only wear hers in a big bun even at the age of five.

"Yes boo boo. Mommy and daddy both have work - a lot of work. In fact, auntie Chloe is going to pick you up," she told her children.

"She's mean, I don't like her," Noel whined.

Farren tapped her thigh with the bottom of the brush. "Watch your mouth," she laughed. It was very much true; Chloe was a prude and had no reason to be. Ever since Christian's father passed, she really hadn't been the same. People don't realize that life has to continue on, even after death.

"Alright now kiddies, it's past midnight; time for bed," Christian came barging in.

"Where is my brother?" Noel asked. She was so much like her mother, full of spunk and personality.

"Sleep, like you're about to be," Christian joked.

"Goodnight ma," Carren, the oldest at fourteen, said.

"Leave that phone in here," Christian instructed.

"Why?" Carren asked, not with attitude but with curiosity.

"Why? I don't have a reason why, I pay the bill. Goodnight boo," he checked her.

Carren looked at her mom for help, and there wasn't much Farren could do. "Come give me a hug. I love you so much. Goodnight, sleep tight," she told her baby.

She mumbled love you too and gave her a church hug. Carren was in that 'I like boys and

I wanna be on the phone all night' stage and her daddy wasn't having it. Noel snuggled under the covers. "What do you think you're doing, Miss Lady?" Farren asked. "Daddy said I could sleep in here," Noel stated.

"Daddy didn't tell mommy this." Farren eyeballed her husband. He winked at her before cutting the light off.

It was nothing new; Noel always slept with them. Carren started off the same way, and then it seemed as if she thought sleeping with mommy and daddy was lame all of a sudden. Noel loved being around Farren; she was her role model. While other five year olds chose Rihanna and Hannah Montana, Noel Sanai Knight wanted to be just like her mommy when she grew up.

The next morning once the children were seen off to school, Christian and Farren talked over coffee. "So what's the plan?" she asked.

"There is no plan. Go to work, enjoy your day, come home, cook dinner and do whatever else you need today." Christian ended the conversation before it could start.

"Don't shut me out," she told him. He inhaled and lit up a blunt. As old as he was beginning to get, smoking weed was therapy for him. When his children were home, he only smoked in the basement or his office. "Babe, I'm not, but what do you want me to say? I got this," he told her.

She huffed and emptied the dishes into the dishwasher. Farren had a long day ahead of her, and arguing with the love of her life was not on her agenda. In her bathroom, she sat at her vanity placing mascara on her eyelashes and eyeliner on her eyelids; those were the only two necessities she needed. Makeup was only worn on special occasions.

Farren decided on a plum, fitted dress with an olive green cardigan, and pearls that derived from the mills in Sierra Leone, Africa. Her and Christian traveled there to celebrate her passing the bar exam.

"You look beautiful," Christian beamed. She rolled her eyes and placed her pearl necklace around her neck. She changed purses and made sure to add her gun. Farren had stopped toting it for a while, but found it necessary again.

"Baby, you don't need that. I hate when you're dramatic," he spat.

"Look, I don't care how you're feeling, but my life is way more important than you thinking you run the fuckin city," Farren gladly let him know.

"Enjoy your day, love." And with that being said, he exited the room.

Christian didn't technically have his wife in the dark but it was a lot she didn't know about him or the life he lived, and for her safety, he chose to keep it that way. He was going to let her think this situation couldn't be handled for the sake of her job. People talked and he knew those federal agents were pussies and would do anything to get her to crack, like jeopardizing her job and etc. Christian had to play his cards the right way, but with one phone call, this case can go bye-bye. Yes people went to jail when you committed crimes and yes it was wrong to sell drugs, but it was never wrong to provide for your family the best way you knew how.

Christian worked hard, lost tons of friends along the way but most importantly, he stayed humble, loyal and paid his dues. Men like Christian Knight paid niggas to handle his dirty work. He was well connected in the city and gave more than enough to local politicians and chiefs. One conversation over lunch with the judge, and he would be scot-free.

The cases they were trying to throw at him were things he did when he was in his prime.

Christian didn't associate himself with anything illegal anymore. He went completely legit for the sake of seeing his children off to prom and graduation.

Christian was outside checking the mail when Farren waltzed past him to enter her car. "I love you boo," he yelled and smirked. He learned to ignore Farren's spoiled ass a very long time ago. She flicked him off and pulled out of the driveway of their million dollar estate.

Upon entering the office, her assistant ran down all of the calls and emails, missed meetings and the office gossip that she thought Farren cared about when she really didn't.

"And you have a visitor who insisted on waiting in your office," she hesitated to say. "Who is it?" she asked before turning the door knob into her corner office.

It was her sister whom she really didn't communicate with. Neeki was still Neeki. Farren gave up years ago on fixing their strained sisterhood. "How can I help you today? Thanks Dolly, I got it from here. Can you get me an iced-caramel coffee, please love?" Farren offered her assistant a warm smile. Over the years, Dolly had become very protective of Farren and shared the hate for Neeki.

"Farren, how have you been? How are the kids? Are you having anymore, anytime soon?" She attempted to make small talk.

"Girl hell no, me and Chrissy are done with children. They're well. Wassup Neeki? I got a busy day," Farren cut through the bullshit.

"You look nice and I love this office." She walked around "admiring" her sister's awards and certificates with envy ever present in her eyes.

"I've been here for seven years; you could've been stopped by. How did you find it anyway?" Farren asked out of curiosity.

"You're famous girl, all I have to do is type your name in Google," she smiled.

"Hard work pays off," Farren let her know without saying much, that she'd put her time in. Despite what her mother and sister thought about her marrying into money, she worked her ass off to be where she is now.

"Soooo, I'm ready to purchase a house and my credit is shot." She finally came out with what she wanted.

"That's great. Christian knows a lot of good real-estate agents; I'll have a few of them send you some houses." Farren scanned her rolodex of business cards and business contacts.

"Farren, I need a loan," Neeki said.

"Oh I can't do that right now. If you want to wait a year or so, then yes, but not right now," Farren told her younger sister.

"And why is that? All that fuckin' money you sitting on and I can't get a hundred thousand dollars?" she asked with sarcasm.

"A hundred thousand? I thought you needed closing costs or something. Neeki, me and Christian are in the middle of a situation and until I can figure out what's going on, I'm not in the position to give away any money, especially a hundred thousand; my husband would kill me if I did that," she shrieked.

"I'm not asking for *his* permission for *your* money," she spat.

"We are one. As I've told you before, it will have to be in a year or so. I'm sorry, but what I can do is refer you to some banks that have programs that work with first-time home buyers," Farren offered in her warmest 'please get the fuck out of my office, I'm busy' voice that she could muster up.

"You are going to need me one day, sis. You need to get off that high horse. You're not perfect." Neeki shook her head and prepared to leave.

"In a year, I can help." Farren didn't like arguing with her sister. She never knew the color of her skin, texture of her hair and that fact that her father was involved in her life would cause her sister so much pain and anger that was directed towards her. In Neeki's eyes, Farren never struggled. She never had to beg or work hard; everything was always handed to her.

When they were younger, Farren slept on a hard, wire mattress that was passed down throughout the family. Farren's father came to visit for one of Farren's track meets in middle school, and flipped out when he saw how his precious daughter was living. Farren's room and closet was instantly upgraded and he threatened to cut the mother's "allowance" if

Farren told him she took her stuff one more
time. Every cell phone he sent, Farren's mother
would sell to buy her a new club dress or
perfume.

Farren always had men at the door, and
she always turned them down; every single one.
Neeki and her mother told her she was stupid
and was going to die alone. Farren knew she
wanted more out of life. She knew she never
wanted to settle or be someone's down time. She
didn't want to be treated like an option. She
wanted to feel and be important; be a Queen.

When Farren was younger she had a wild
and crazy love affair with an older man. It led to
years of fights with his wife and even his
children. Farren never left though. As much as
she tried to convince herself that Dice's death
wasn't to teach her a lesson, she knew in the
back of her mind that if he would have never
been murdered, she probably would still be that

young ,lost girl searching for love; love she desperately wanted to come from her parents.

Farren attempted to get as much work done as possible, but her mind was in scrambles. Dolly entered her office. "Girl, what are you still doing here?" Farren had sent her home around 6 p.m. "I didn't want you here by yourself, and plus I need a ride home," she giggled. Farren shook her head and powered off her laptop. She slid her feet into her Tory slides. Being on heels all day was a little too much for her.

"Come on Dolly Dolly," she joked as they went to the garage. Perched up on her truck was a detective from earlier. Farren pulled her gun from the bottom of the bag to the top. "Don't make us come for you," he said and walked off.

Her heartbeat quickened. "Get in the car, Dolly," she instructed. Once they were in the car and on the highway, Farren leaned her head back and took a deep breath. "Is everything okay?" Dolly asked.

"Girl, it will be," she told her.

"Do you want to come in and have a drink?" Dolly offered. Farren always told her no when she invited her places, but made sure she always sent a gift and such.

"You know what, tonight I need that drink." She took the key out of the ignition, and entered the home.

"Dolly, I haven't been here since you closed; you have made this place look amazing," she told her assistant in awe.

"Mrs. Knight, I'm so grateful for everything you and Mr. Knight have done for me and my girls," she said. "Anytime Dolly, you know we love you," she touched her hand and tipped her glass.

"Mrs. Knight, what's going on?" she asked after they damn near downed a fifth of Hennessy.

She ran her hands over her face and placed stray hairs behind her ear. "My husband... his old life has caught up with him and we might be facing some serious ass charges if he doesn't handle it," she admitted.

"Are you for real?" she asked.

Farren nodded her head and sipped her drink. "Are you going to leave him?" she asked.

Farren looked at her and laughed. "Girl, we done been through worst shit than this. No, I'll never leave Christian. He is my best friend. I'll take those charges if he asked me to," she told Dolly.

"You would? But why?" she asked. She looked to Farren as a role model and a big sister. To hear her say she would throw her family and career away was very, very shocking.

"Have you ever been in love?" Farren asked.

Dolly thought before answering. "I'm twenty-two. I had my daughters when I was fourteen and sixteen. I don't think I knew what love was then. I can't even find my children's daddies to collect child support."

"Don't be looking for them; raise your kids yourself. You don't need them Dolly," Farren yelled.

"I've never been in love, though. I'm always so busy with work and school, I don't even have time for a relationship," she told her boss.

"You remind so much of me when I was your age. I worked two full-time jobs, was in law school, I didn't date, didn't give my number out; girl I was the devil. My husband caught me on a good night," she reminisced.

"How did you know he was the one?" she was curious.

"Dolly, I made my husband wait so long to have sex with me it was ridiculous. Sex isn't how I know he loved me, but he was patient and attentive. We both had broken hearts and cared for each other; we felt each other's spirits. I can never stay mad at Christian long. He pushes me when I want to give up on myself," Farren smiled and thought about her personal blessing.

"I hope I find that one day," Dolly said.

"You will girl, when you least expect it. I'mma hook you up though," she told her.

"My husband has called me three times. Let me get home before he has everyone looking for me." She gathered her belongings.

"We're going to the spa Saturday. Bring the kids to my house; my daughter will watch them. I'll text you the address," she said before she pulled off.

When she got in her car, she called Christian's cell. "Babe, where ya at? We at mama's house," he said loudly into the phone. I heard everyone in the background laughing.

"Where are my kids," she asked.

"They're here. You know Chloe got them from school," he responded.

"I'm on the way, boo," Farren told her husband before disconnecting the call.

Family time at Christian's mother house was always a big deal. Farren loved being over there because she didn't have this growing up.

"Mommmmyyyyyyyyyyyy," Noel screamed when she saw her mother walk through the door.

"Hi baby, I've been missing you all day." Farren tickled her tummy. She didn't want Noel to grow up.

"I missed you more. Daddy bought pizza. You want me to fix you some?" she asked. Noel was always being a help around the house. "Yes baby," she said, tussling her hair.

Christian called her into the living room, and she flopped in his lap. "You've been drinking?" he whispered into her ear as he rubbed her back.

"Long day, boo," she told him. He looked in her eyes asking mental questions. He nodded his head. "Where wa..." Noel bombarded her parents with a slice of pepperoni pizza for her mother. "Thanks boo. Go get your stuff and tell your auntie thank you for picking you up," she told her daughter.

"They came to my job," she told him before he could ask any more questions. "I'm okay, baby. Dolly was with me; her car is back in the shop. I'm thinking about giving her that Lexus that's at the other house. We were saving it for Carren, but I'mma get my baby any car she wants. Her grades are excellent," she told her husband. He nodded. She knew Christian's head was probably everywhere right now.

He got up and his phone fell onto the couch. She started to call out to him, but the text message on the phone didn't have any content just the name, "Asia."

"Who the fuck is Asia?" Farren asked when she found her husband in the basement.

"Don't come down here questioning me, and give me my phone," he snatched it from her hands.

"I'm not doing this with you tonight, tomorrow, or next week, so nip that shit in the bud ASAP." She clapped her hands and left him alone in the basement and took her children home.

Christian

Farren was a firecracker for no reason. She was dramatic and she dragged out every situation. He remembered the second year after they were married.

Ashley was visiting and she was at home with her children. She saw his old assistant in his bathroom, fixing her makeup.

"How was it?" she asked the girl. Farren was dressed nicely, leaving from work or class. She leaned on the bathroom door.

"Excuse me?" the assistant responded.

"My husband's dick....was it good to you?" she asked.

She laughed and attempted to exit the bathroom. Farren closed the bathroom door and mushed her in the head, and then held her chin in her hand firmly. "You won't be nothing more than bathroom and office sex, is that what you want to do with your life? If I ask him to fire you he will, so your best bet is to come do your job and go home, bitch," she told the girl.

He laughed in his father's basement after he thought back to that crazy ass day.

Farren didn't condone cheating, and it wasn't much Christian was able to get away with. He seemed to forget that his precious wife knew every lie and made up story in the book; she was a man's downtime for six years.

Her last run-in was about three years ago, and Farren told Christian she wouldn't be disrespected any longer. He was spending an awful lot of time at the strip club and Farren didn't understand why. He had a brick house at home for a wife, and it was all natural. Farren was constantly pulling tricks out of an elephant's ass to please her husband, so what made him step out made her completely clueless. That night she called his phone a million times and no answer. Christian's friends all were very active on Myspace. Her husband hated social media. She was able to locate him making it rain in a VIP section.

She was dressed in leather pants, red Chanel heels and a wife beater with her red mink. It was two weeks before Christmas and one day before they were to take the children to California to do some early shopping. Christian should have been home packing his shit for their family trip. Farren tiptoed through the club, looking and feeling like a million bucks. In his lap sat some stripper hoe that her associates from the hood told her Christian had been feeling the last few months. Greg, Christian's best friend tapped Christian's shoulder, but it was too late. Farren had the young hoe by her weave and on the floor with her foot in her chest. Christian knew better, so he sat there thinking his wife was fuckin crazy and obsessed with him. "He won't leave me, you know why? 'Cause my pussy isn't tarnished. He knows it's his. Yours? It's for anyone in here *with the biggest bank. Don't waste your time sweetie." She pulled her up. "Now you? You need to beat me home. I'm thirty-seven, you think this what the fuck I wanna do with my time?" she asked him quietly. The girl came from behind with a bottle, and Christian rose up. "Asia chill girl, what the fuck is wrong with you?" he yelled.*

"Get this bitch, Chris. You gon' let her put her feet on my face?" she wailed.

"Get this bitch? You mean get your wife, who gave him his children, who he sleeps with every night, who pussy he eats before he brushes his teeth. Baby, don't play yourself." She tossed her hand to dismiss her.

"You think you got something because you have a ring? Bitch, you still not shit. Hoe wassup?!" the stripper popped her shit. Christian shushed her. "Asia, chill please," he attempted to hush her.

"Christian, I don't want you in here anymore,"
she made herself clear.

The next morning they managed to fake it for the
children but after dinner and shopping in Los
Angeles, Farren told him as they prepared for
bed, "I love you and I love our children, but I will
not compromise my happiness because you can't
keep your dick in pants," as tears streamed
down her face. Christian didn't say anything; he
never did. He stripped naked and entered the
shower. She left him in the bathroom with his
thoughts and cried herself to sleep.

"Ma, I'm about to leave; come lock the
door." Christian snapped out of the flashbacks
and prepared to go home.

"Okay son, thanks for bringing dinner,"
she said. He loved his mother and would do
anything for her. After his father died, they were
all scared that she would be depressed and sad
but she appeared to be full of joy, knowing her
husband was no longer in pain.

"Have you talked to Courtney?" his mother asked.

He shook his head. "I'll go over there tomorrow." She looked at him with the "don't play with me" eyes.

"Night ma, love you," he told her.

"Christian, don't lose your family over two hours of temporary fun." She patted his back and closed the door.

Christian pulled up into his home, and crashed the engine. He entered through the garage and saw his son still playing video games. "Aye boy, get in the tub and get in the bed," he told him.

Michael was his pride and joy. He loved his son. "I got somebody tryna get you that PS4, too, son," he told him before he entered the bedroom he shared with his wife.

She was drying her hair. Her golden blonde hair graced the crack of her ass, so long and curly. Christian loved to stare at Farren naked. He placed all four of his cell phones on the nightstand, and removed his cufflinks, wallet and gun.

She slid on a t-shirt and got into bed. "Farren, it's too much going on right now for you to have an attitude," he told her.

She looked up at him. "Fuck you Christian. You don't think I wouldn't remember who Asia was?" she yelled.

"Lower your voice, our kids are not asleep," he hissed.

"I'm sorry, but tonight I'm not pretending everything is perfect. Kids, your daddy is a cheating ass bastard that would rather risk losing us to be with some fuckin two-dollar hoe," she yelled, and tears ran down her face. She was beet red. Her emotions mixed in with the liquor had Farren going from zero to one-hundred real quick.

Michael came in the room. "Ma, why are you crying?" Noel peeped around the door as well. "Y'all go to sleep," I told my children.

"Ma, what's wrong?" my son ignored me.

"Get in the bed and go to sleep and say your prayers," he told them again.

They did not budge. Farren held her stomach as tears poured out from her soul. Even if she was hurt, our children did not have to sec that she was so fuckin dramatic sometimes.

"I'm okay babies," she managed to say.

Carren came in and got them. "Come on y'all." She closed our door.

I threw a pillow at her. "I hate when you act like the fuckin' world is ending. Stop that shit! I'm here now, ain't I?" I told her.

"But can you honestly say this is where you want to be?" she asked, fear ever so present in her eyes. Farren asked the question but was unsure if she wanted the answer. To others it may have appeared as if they had the perfect love story, but sometimes she didn't know what this was or what they were doing. The same man that made her feel like the luckiest girl on earth also made her feel so insecure. Farren believed she was beautiful, she knew she was a good mother, but money cannot buy loyalty, money cannot buy happiness and it cannot make your husband's dick stay in his pants. In their years of being together, she never wavered, never even thought of men besides her ex who was dead and gone. She was completely in love with her husband and no one could take that away.

The next morning was a blur. Farren ran for her life. She did her morning routine as she normally does, but an irritated feeling in the pit of her stomach was saying, *something is not right.* She turned up her Beyoncé and continued on with her run. When she stopped to take a break and to decrease her heart rate, a man in a black suit was standing near a tree. It wasn't too often you'd see African-Americans in this prestigious neighborhood. With all of this shit going on, Farren was stupid to run without her phone or gun.

She kept her eye on him as she jogged in place, and cracked her neck. Before she knew it, the man was coming out of hiding and Farren took off down the hill, running for her life. Out of nowhere, two more men snatched her up, and before she could scream, a dirty un-manicured hand covered her mouth, forcing her to be silent...

To be Continued

Made in the USA
Lexington, KY
15 May 2015